MARION CATTERALL

LET LOVE BE MY JUDGE

DIAMOND MEDIA PRESS CO.
1-304-273-6157
https://www.diamondmediapressco.com/

ISBN Paperback: 9781951302535

Contents

Chapter 1: My Story Begins. 1

Chapter 2: America 7

Chapter 3: Back Home 35

Chapter 4: First Visit..39

Chapter 5: Returning to Normality...49

Chapter 6: Second Visit...53

Chapter 7: Home Again 63

Chapter 8: Las Vegas 89

Chapter 9: A New Start 103

Chapter 10: Decision Time..171

Acknowledgements

To my dearest husband, William; my two sons, David and Stephen; and to my three beautiful girls, Jennifer, Clare, and Sarah, with all my love and affection.

Chapter 1
My Story Begins.

My name is Catherine Riding, and this is my story. I had just celebrated my fortieth birthday, and the Christmas and the New Year celebrations had finished. It was a bleak, cold January evening, and I asked my family to be good enough to spare some time in the lounge after our evening meal rather than disappear to their rooms or go out to meet friends. I wanted us all to discuss and choose the next family holiday, which hopefully would be the following July. The day before, I had raided all the local travel agencies for as many holiday brochures I could find.

As a family, we had suffered over the two previous years. I thought of them as years from hell. They had put us on an emotional roller coaster with heartache, worry, and stress. That is why I thought it would be wonderful if we could all have a family holiday as Tony, our son, who was twenty-one years old, and our two daughters, Carol, who was eighteen years old, and Jennifer, who was sixteen years old, probably would not be interested in a family holiday after this year.

Over the past two years, my husband, Richard, had suffered many health issues. He had been seriously ill on more than one occasion— two heart attacks, a triple bypass, serious lung disease, a vascular disease, cancer, and chronic rheumatoid arthritis, which he had always suffered from. Obviously, he was unfit to work, but he always stayed happy and positive.

Our son, Tony, had, over the two previous years, been made redundant and had suffered a negative effect from a weekend taking recreational drugs that had left him with severe depression. And one occasion, when life seemed far too much for him, had resulted in an overdose of tablets. Thank goodness he survived, and he was being treated with all the psychiatric help he needed to help him get his life back on track. He was six foot four inches tall, but he was my baby.

Our younger daughter, Jennifer, had not escaped the bad luck of the previous two years. After being clipped by a speeding car on her way home from school, she had suffered two broken legs. Again, she was lucky to have healed perfectly with only the memories of that fateful afternoon left.

Years before, my husband and I had started a haulage business. Over the years, we had seen it grow into a fleet of twelve, thirty-tonne wagons. As my husband's health failed, he worked less and less, which meant that I worked more and more. The previous two years had seen the recession hit us. Like many other businesses, we struggled to keep trading. I was working full time then. I was constantly robbing Peter to pay Paul. As most of our debtors were closing their doors and going into receivership, our cash flow was so badly hit that I ended up having to finish some of our workforce. My choices were not easy— either sell the vehicles or park them up, borrow money to help us pay the weekly wages bill, and in most cases, run up our debts to our creditors. At the end of some weeks, we could not even afford to pay ourselves. The worry was constant. I could not sleep at night, but we fought on. At last, we had now seen the worst of the recession, and the business was now ticking over quite nicely.

How I managed to stay calm, firm, and positive over that terrible time, I will never know. I was a strong person, and I could take the rough with the smooth. I had a good, happy nature, and I could hide my feelings pretty well.

I had, over the previous two years, undergone two hip re-placements. The left replacement had gone well, but the right replacement developed some complications resulting in the hip not being able to hold much weight. I needed help with steps and gradients as well as getting in and out of chairs or in and out of cars. Otherwise, I was in really good health, and I was looking forward to a brighter future.

My husband and I did not have an intimate relationship. His ill health and medication meant that he was impotent. This had never been an issue for me, as I had never been interested in sex. It had never really appealed to me, and the older I be-came, the less sex was part of my life.

I was quite tall and slim, and I considered myself to be quite attractive. I had blond hair and blue-green eyes. I loved beautiful clothes and jewellery. I never went out of the house without my make-up on and my nails done to perfection.

I had been educated to a high standard, having attended a convent school, an all-girls school, until I was eighteen. In later life, and while we built up the haulage business, I qualified as a company accountant.

***

A roaring fire in the lounge was there to greet us all. I looked at each member of my family, so proud that we had all pulled together and survived the worst. I just wanted us all to have a special summer holiday together to celebrate our resilience and to celebrate that life was looking good for us all, at last.

We all had views as to what kind of holiday would be good. We laughed at some of the suggestions. We talked at length about the proposed holiday, and after an hour or so, and after all the holiday brochures had been read, we made a final decision.

America was to be the destination. Florida was to be the area. We planned a two-centre holiday; that is, one week in Orlando and one week in Miami. Orlando would provide us with nonstop entertainment, restaurants galore, sunshine, bars, and nightclubs. Miami, on the other hand, would provide us with rest, beach, sea, sunshine, and restaurants.

All done! The very next day, I was down at the travel agents booking everything that my family had chosen the night before. *Fantastic!* I thought to myself. *We all need something to look forward to.* We had chosen the month of June, so we had quite a while to wait for that holiday, but it soon arrived.

We made use of the waiting time to shop for new clothing and all the holiday essentials like sunscreen lotions. I arranged time off work and employed a driver who was used to running the office and was extremely good at administrative work. No problem there then.

Chapter 2
America

The departure day arrived at last. We all checked in at the airport, bordered our plane, and settled down for the long-haul flight to Orlando. It went so quickly, and in no time at all, we disembarked the plane, collected the hire car, and headed for our accommodation for the week. A sat nav was as a standard feature on the hire car. Without that sat nav, goodness knows where we would have ended up!

What a place Orlando was! It was fantastic, awesome, and brilliant – a never-ending menu of delights that serviced the mind and the body. We literally could have spent a year there and still not seen and experienced everything on offer. Every day, we would set off after a good breakfast and return late at night exhausted.

The night-time entertainment did not fail us. We enjoyed

nightly firework displays, shows, music, and dancing. There was an abundance of restaurants to choose from, and the food was second to none.

After saying all that, we were all ready for our journey to Miami. We were all in need of rest and relaxation.

The drive to Miami proved to be a few hours' drive. We had flown into Orlando, and our return flight was to leave via Miami airport in a week's time. By the time we had found our accommodation in Miami, we were literally fed up and tired.

The next day, all of us rested. Then, finally fed and watered, we realized what a beautiful place we had come to. The hotel, like so many other hotels, was situated on the beachfront. Each hotel had its own beach-side frontage complete with beach bars and swimming pools. We all settled down to enjoy the sand, sea, and sunshine.

Our accommodation was superb. It was comprised of two rooms with an adjoining door. Each room had two large, queen-size beds, but the logistics of our sleeping arrangements meant that my husband and I would have to share with our two daughters while our son had a room to himself. The adjoining door was always left ajar or open, making our rooms spacious, handy, and comfortable.

During the day, my husband and I rested on sunbeds by the pool. I was not one for the sand, although we did spend some time on the beach. We just left Tony, Carol, and Jennifer to do their own thing.

In the evening, after showering and dressing, we would all go out together to eat an evening meal, sometimes in the hotel restaurant, and sometimes, at one of the many beach-front bars. We were spoilt for choice, and we could not fault the local cuisine. After an evening meal, my husband and I, with our two daughters, would walk along the boardwalk admiring the many bars, each decorated with thousands of small coloured lights. Music drifted from one bar to the next. It was quite a magical place, and we enjoyed such a feel-good factor. At this point, Tony would leave us to join people of his own age group who congregated on the beach beside tin barrels containing good, large fires. Most nights, Tony had had too much to drink by the time he returned to his room, usually around three o'clock in the morning. Who was I to try and say anything to him as, at the age of twenty-one, even in America, he was at a legal age to drink alcoholic beverages?

We were on day five of our week in Miami. After the usual day in the sun, resting and swimming, we all met at our rooms to shower and dress for the evening meal. As usual, when we were ready, we all made our way to the boardwalk and settled in a lovely, lively restaurant to eat.

As Tony finished his meal and was about to leave us to join his newfound friends, I said, 'Tony, please be careful. I don't want you having too much to drink. Just be sensible.'

'Stop worrying, Mum. I know when to stop drinking.' This was his reply. With that said, he left in a hurry.

'Leave the lad alone!' said my husband. 'He has only a couple of days left. Let him enjoy himself.'

My husband and I, with our two daughters, made our way back to our hotel. We had had such a lovely day, and we were all very tired. The girls were asleep in no time, and Richard and I sat on the balcony watching the world go by.

As the night air became colder, we retired to our bed, curled up, and went to sleep.

I was awakened by the sound of the adjoining door being locked. *Why has Tony locked the door?* I thought to myself. I waited, trying to hear anything from Tony's room. Everything seemed quiet, so I fell back to sleep.

Quite a while later, I was awakened by the sound of banging. It sounded as if furniture in Tony's room was being moved around or even being damaged. I woke Richard and told him, so he knocked on the adjoining door. There was no reply.

'Tony, are you all right in there?' I shouted at the closed door. Still no answer.

The noises coming from his room sounded as if there was a fight happening. I was getting very frightened, and I shouted even louder, 'Open this door now! Answer me, Tony. Are you all right? What is happening in there?' Still no answer.

I ran into the hallway, and I was horrified to find that police officers were in the hallway and also in Tony's room. There was a lot of shouting and pushing, and I could not get past the two officers who were blocking my way.

'Go back to your room, ma'am. There is nothing for you to see here,' one officer shouted at me. He continued to shout, 'Get back to your room now!'

At this point, I saw a glimpse of Tony being dragged, handcuffed, out of his room. I screamed, 'What is happening? Where are you taking him?'

'I told you before – get back to your room. There is nothing to see here,' the officer shouted at me. He then physically pushed me back towards my room door.

'Don't you push me!' I shouted even louder. 'I want to know what is happening to my son. I want to know where you are taking him and why!'

'So you are the mother,' said one of the police officers. 'Go back to your room as you have been told to do, and I will arrange for someone to come and talk to you.'

I ran back into our room, where Richard was waiting with Carol and Jennifer.

'The police have dragged him out of his room, and they have taken him away!' I cried to Richard. 'I don't know why! And I don't know where they have taken him.' I started to cry with fear and frustration. 'They said they will send someone to talk to us, but when?' I added.

I waited until the police had finished in Tony's room, and then I went into the room. It looked as if there had been some kind of fight. I placed Tony's clothes in his travel bag and found his passport and travel documents to keep safe for him. I unlocked the adjoining door, and then, with Richard and the girls, I waited for someone to come and tell us what the hell was going on. Nobody came! I was now becoming quite frightened. Richard suggested that we go down to reception to see if they knew what was happening.

As we came out of the lift, we were met by the police officers. They would not talk to us, and as I looked outside, I could see Tony sitting in a police car. At this point, I just lost it. 'I demand that someone comes to talk to my husband and me!' I shouted. 'This is unacceptable! Will someone please tell us why my son is being held in that police car!'

A few moments later, a smart-looking, middle-aged gentleman came over to us and asked us to sit down and calm down. 'Your son has been arrested and charged with the rape of a young woman,' he said in a matter-of-fact manner. He continued, 'The girl in question has been taken to the rape crisis center for an examination. We are to wait here until she returns, and then your son will be taken to Miami-Dade County Pre-Trial Detention Center to be formerly charged. Bail will be set then.'

'This is nonsense,' I said, trying to keep composed. 'How do I know where he is being taken and how much the bail will be? And where would we pay the bail?'

'Someone will contact you. What is your telephone number?' he asked.

'We only have our room telephone number. Our room is

1064. That's the only point of contact you'll have for us, and we have that only for today and tomorrow, as we are supposed to be leaving and flying home the day after.'

'Sorry, I can't guarantee that anyone will call you in that time frame. You'll need to leave a forwarding telephone number when you vacate your room,' said the police official.

When I looked out of the window, the police car holding Tony had gone. I was in shock. I could not think what I should do. Richard was visibly shaken, and Carol and Jennifer just sat and cried.

'I will have to sit by our room phone and wait for someone to contact us. I don't know what else to do,' I said to Richard. 'Take the girls out for something to eat and then take them to the swimming pool for the rest of the day. If I hear anything, I'll come and find you.' I was trying not to seem too concerned in front of the girls.

I waited most of the day, hoping and praying that someone would contact me. It was late in the afternoon when I finally received a phone call from the courthouse. I was informed that Tony had been formerly charged with raping a girl who was eighteen years old. I asked what was to happen next, and I was told that a bail bondsman would probably contact me and that bail had been set at ten thousand dollars. I was told that Tony was to be held at the Miami- Dade County Pre-Trial Detention-Center.

Within minutes of that conversation with the person at the courthouse, I answered the phone to a Mr. Chris Maloney who introduced himself as a bail bondsman. 'Good afternoon. Am I speaking to the mother of a Mr. Tony Riding?' he asked.

'Yes, you are,' I replied. I had so many questions to ask him, but he continued, 'Bail has been set at ten thousand dollars. Do you have a credit card with that amount in available funds?' he asked.

'No, unfortunately, we have not. What can we use instead of a credit card? How else can I pay the bail? When I pay, will my son be released to me until a trial date?' I asked. I had so many more questions, but this Mr. Chris Maloney was only interested in the money immediately from the security of a credit card. I continued, 'Please help me, Mr. Maloney. I am at a loss with the American legal system. Help me, or at least advise me as to how I can get the money for the bail paid and what happens next.'

'The courts will take cash or money orders. You will need to arrange a money transfer to a post office here and withdraw the money in money orders. It will have to be done, and the bail paid before the arraignment hearing tomorrow morning, as the court may increase the amount of bail once the charges are made formally.' This was Mr. Maloney's answer.

'I will do that with immediate effect,' I told him. 'I shall contact my sister and arrange for her to transfer the required money to a designated post office here, and I shall withdraw it in money orders.' I took a deep breath. 'Will you help me pay it to the court to release my son before the arraignment? Please leave me your phone number, and as soon as I have secured the money orders, I shall contact you. Hopefully, by then, I will be able to meet you and pay the bail to the court. Would you do that for me and my family? We have no one else to ask for help.'

With that, he agreed and gave me his mobile phone number.

My poor sister, Margaret, and her husband, Matt! Not only was I telling her the bad news about the trouble Tony had got himself in, but I was also asking her to raise and release ten thousand dollars, sending it to us by wiring it to a designated post office in Miami. This, she agreed to do. With any luck, I would receive it early the next morning. I contacted Chris Maloney and arranged to meet him outside the courthouse as soon as I had collected the money orders.

That night, I could not sleep. All I wanted to do was secure Tony's release. Then, within hours, we would all be on the plane flying back home. I would worry about the charges and dates for a trial when we were all safe and sound back home.

The next morning, we were in a race against time. We had to locate the designated post office, give them the unique pass code, collect the money in money orders, and hurry to meet Chris Maloney in front of the courthouse. We did all of this only to find that Tony's arraignment was over. The county court judge, Thomas Hague, had increased Tony's bail to one hundred thousand dollars and sentenced him to the detention center until such time as a hearing was to be heard.

We were all devastated. My husband was visibly shaken, our daughters were crying, and I was numb with shock. How could I go home and leave my son in America, awaiting legal action for a crime he did not commit? I knew he had not committed the crime of rape. I knew my son better that anyone in the whole world. Without thinking twice, I pushed my way into the courtroom, pulling my daughters with me. I stood in front of the judge's bench, and I asked Judge Thomas Hague to listen to me. This was not a good move on my part, but I was desperate and was not thinking straight.

'Madam, you must leave this courtroom now,' demanded the judge, 'or you will be removed forcefully and maybe arrested yourself for the disruption you are causing in this court!'

'You have just heard the case against my son, Tony Riding,' I explained. 'There must be a mistake here somewhere—'

But before I could finish my sentence, Judge Hague said, 'I know the case you refer to. Your son is charged with a very serious offence – the rape of a young woman. He is obviously a flight risk, and because of this, I have increased the bail to one hundred thousand dollars.' He turned to an officer of the court. 'Remove this woman and her family from this court room!' he shouted.

***

Back in our hotel room, my husband and I now had to decide what had to be done next. Early the following morning, our flight was due to take us all back home. We decided that, because of my husband's health issues, he would return to England with our daughters and that I would remain in Miami. We packed all our belongings and vacated our rooms. I drove my husband and our daughters to the airport so they could fly home, and I arranged to keep the hire car for a while longer. I set off back to the central area of Miami to find another accommodation for myself, but that proved nearly impossible. The coming July Fourth – Independence Day – celebrations had caused every available room to be occupied. In desperation, I returned to our original hotel and pleaded with them for help in finding a place for me to stay. Their answer to my pleas was to offer me a basement worker's accommodation. Although it did not have a phone, I accepted their offer, moved in, and unpacked my cases.

I spent most of the night trying to work out what I could do next. I needed a lawyer, but how did I find one? I needed to speak to the British Consulate. I had tried, but my calls had just gone to an answer machine, and I had no phone number to leave them so they could contact me. I needed an appointment with them. Tony's clothes, medicines, toiletries, money, and passport were there with me. I had to try and get them to him, even the sunscreen lotions that he would need if he was to be outside for any length of time. Who could help me? From the hotel's reception phone, I tried to phone Chris Maloney, the bail bond person, but he would not answer my calls. The only other person in all of America with whom I'd had contact was the Honourable Judge Thomas Hague. So be it. I would have to do my best to get him to help me, or at least put me in contact with someone who could help me.

The next morning, I drove to the detention center and asked how could I arrange a visit with my son. I asked if they could take his bags from me and make sure he received them as he would really need them. They did not want to know. The only advice I was given was to take on a lawyer who would handle all of my instructions. Again, how was I to find a good lawyer?

I parked my hire car in the centre of Miami. I walked and walked until I found the chambers of the Honourable Judge Thomas Hague. I had looked him up and learned that his chambers and offices were in an old building attached to the courthouse.

I stood outside the offices for what seemed such a long time. I had no idea what I should do. I felt completely lost, and I was very tired. It was only the middle of the afternoon, but when I finally tried the doors to the offices, they were closed and locked.

I decided to return to my car and make my way back to the basement room at the hotel. I was very tired, and I needed to sleep and gather my thoughts so I could figure out what I was going to do to help my son. I had no idea how I was going to find a good lawyer, especially as I had no phone and did not know anyone at all in this town – no, not just this town, but in America itself. I tried to purchase a mobile phone only to be told that I needed an American bank account for the payments that would be required. I had to give up on that idea. I had no phone in my basement room, so, all in all, I felt totally defeated. The only person that I knew – and that was by name only – was the Honourable Judge Thomas Hague. He was the judge who had remanded my son to the detention center and increased his bail from the ten thousand dollars to one hundred thousand dollars. There was no way I could raise that sort of cash.

As I turned around to walk back to my hire car, I noticed a side entrance to the building that housed the chambers and offices. It was slightly ajar. I went to investigate and opened the door further. In I went. In front of me was a large stair well. I walked up the stairs until I found a door that was open. I walked through. I was then on an office corridor. I walked a little further, and I could see through glass doors. To my relief, I could see Judge Hague sitting at a desk.

I knocked politely before I walked straight in to his office.

'I do apologize for this unannounced visit, Judge, but I really need to speak with you. Just give me five minutes of your time so I can explain what a dilemma I am in. I am hoping you can help me—'

But before I could finish my sentence, he stood up and demanded that I leave immediately. 'Leave now, or I will call security and have you escorted from this building. How the hell did you get in unannounced? Get out of my office!' he shouted.

I stood there looking at him. His eyes met mine, and I felt such a jolt of sexual electricity run all through my body. It took me by surprise, and I felt myself blushing.

I dropped Tony's bags to the floor, and I held my head up

high. I kept his gaze and continued. 'Just listen to me for five minutes. I have seen my husband and children onto a plane to return home, so I am now on my own in a strange place with no proper accommodation, no phone, no contacts, and no one I can ask for help—'

He then rudely interrupted me again: 'Leave now or I will have you arrested!'

'Good, then I will be able to see my son and give him his belongings, which I have here. I went to the detention center, and guess what? They would not give me the time of day. The advice I was given was to find a lawyer who would make sure that my son received his belongings – things he desperately needs, like his shoes, toiletries, and so forth. How the hell do I find a lawyer if no one is prepared to help me?' I said, talking through my teeth.

As he sat back down, he buzzed his secretary and asked her to call security.

I looked him straight in the eyes again. That strong sexual attraction feeling hit me again – all through my body. With my head held high and still talking through my teeth, I continued talking as fast as I could. 'Your Honour, sir, you who cannot be approached … you who call yourself Your Honour … well you are far from honourable! You do not deserve to be in that position. I asked you for five minutes! It was you who sentenced my son by raising the bail. The least you could do is listen to me!'

Two security guards entered the room and started towards me as I stood my ground. To my surprise, Judge Thomas Hague dismissed them. I watched him as he spoke to the security men. He was tall with darkish skin and very dark eyes. He was very handsome. His hair was also dark. He had a good physique, and he was wearing a large stud diamond earring in one ear.

When the security men left and closed the door, the judge said to me, 'Lose the attitude!' He remained seated, looking at me from head to toe. I could feel his eyes on me, and again, I felt electricity zapping through my body. I felt embarrassed and angry with myself for feeling this way. 'You have five minutes, so you had better start talking, and as I said before, lose the attitude!'

I took a deep breath and started my speech: 'I am on my own in a strange town – and strange country – with no phone, and the only accommodation I could get was a basement room because of the July Fourth holiday. The room does not have a phone. I am in need of an appointment with a good lawyer. I also need someone to contact the British Counsulate and make an appointment for them to see me. All this is so urgent. I do not want to wait until the end of the holiday period. I need to get my son's belongings to him. He needs his shoes and other important things. I tried to obtain a mobile phone, but that was impossible. You were the only person I knew by name who could possibly help me or who could give me the name of someone who could.' I took a deep breath and continued. 'I had arranged and collected ten thousand dollars for my son's release, but you increased the bail. I am now left with this amount of money in money orders. I have my son's passport. What do I do with this?' I had said all that I could say. I continued to look straight into eyes. I continued to feel the sexual energy between us. I was tired and weary, and I turned to pick up my son's belongings.

'Leave those,' he said. 'I will make sure your son gets them today.' He continued to speak in a calm voice, a soothing voice. 'You should not be carrying your passports and money around with you, especially in Miami. Give me your two passports and the money orders, and I will arrange to have them taken to your hotel later today. I will do my best to arrange the two appointments that you require. I will send someone with all of this at seven this evening. Wait in the reception area, and someone will bring you what you need.'

As I handed him the passports and money orders, our hands touched. It was only for a brief moment, but there was no denying that we had some very strong sexual connection. I jumped back and made a quick exit through the office next door. I was relieved that the ordeal was over. I never thanked him, and I was not going to. I exited the building and made my way back to the hire car. Not long after that, I was so relieved to be back in my little basement room.

As I glanced in the mirror on the wall, I was horrified to see just what a mess I looked. I always try to look good, but today, I looked like an old, middle-aged woman. Seeing that, I showered, washed my hair, dressed in a beautiful dress, and I dried my hair. With the full complement of jewellery, silk stockings, and make-up, I looked like a middle-aged woman with swollen eyes. I laughed at myself, but I did look better, and that made me feel better. I rested with a cup of coffee and recalled everything that had happened that day.

At seven o'clock, I made my way to the foyer of the hotel and made myself comfortable on one of the large sofas. As I looked through the front windows, I saw a large white Mercedes car pull in and park up in the car park. I knew before I saw the driver that it would be Judge Thomas Hague himself.

He entered the hotel and glanced around the foyer. He seemed a little surprised when he saw me sitting there. 'You look rested and better than you did earlier,' he said, smiling.

'Maybe,' I said. 'I still feel helpless, worried, and disgusted at what has happened to my son.' My voice still sounded angry.

'I have told you before, lose the attitude and listen to what I have managed to do for you.' He handed me a slip of paper. 'On this paper is information about an appointment I have made you with a lawyer – Stephen Hewell – at nine thirty tomorrow morning. All his details are there for you.' He handed me another paper. 'On this paper is information about an appointment with Mrs. Margaret Hayes at the British Consulate in Miami. Again, all the details are there for you.' He handed me a third piece of paper. 'On this paper is the booking for accommodations at the Holiday Inn, which is next door to the consulate. Across from the Holiday Inn is a Wendy's restaurant. At least you can just walk there for your food. With that, my job is done.' He bowed and laughed.

I was so surprised and most grateful. I laughed with him for a moment, but the laugh soon turned to tears. I composed myself and thanked him for everything he had done. I placed all the papers, money orders, and passports into the envelope that he had brought them in, and the judge took them to the reception desk and asked them to keep the envelope safe for me.

'How long has it been since your last meal?' the judge asked.

'I cannot remember, as I do not feel hungry,' I replied.

'Come with me now,' he said. 'I have a table booked to have a meal. You can have something to eat, and then I will bring you back. You need to rest tonight as you have a very long day ahead of you tomorrow, but you should have plenty of time for everything. After you have seen Mr. Hewell, you will see Mrs. Hayes at the consulate. Insist there and then that she arranges for you to speak to your son. If I were you, I would refuse to leave until you have permission to speak to him. She has the authority to arrange all this for you,' said the judge, looking straight into my eyes at all times.

'I don't know what to say to you,' I said quietly.

'Say you will come and eat with me,' he said.

'I sometimes need a little help getting up from chairs, in and out of cars, and up steps,' I said, 'because my right leg cannot hold my weight properly.' I felt so stupid having to mention that, but the judge seemed okay with it and nodded.

'Come on then,' he said, smiling at me.

I held onto his arm as he helped me up from the sofa. What a delicious feeling I felt. We got into his car, and I struggled to fasten my safety belt. Feeling stupid again, I had to ask him to help me. As he leaned across me to clip the belt in, I could feel his breath against my face, and with no warning, his lips were just touching mine. He backed away and then came back with a sensual kiss. Wow! I thought. I smiled at him, and he backed away and then came back with a heavy, hard, and urgent kiss. This time, I put my arms around his neck and kissed him back. He jumped out of the car, came round to my passenger side, opened the door, fastened my belt, closed the door, and got back into the driving seat.

'That was most inappropriate. I apologize. Most inappropriate,' he said.

We drove in silence, and before long, we had entered a long drive leading to the Gold Golf Club and Spa. The clubhouse was huge and beautiful, with white pillars across the front of the old building. The judge parked up and came to help me out of the car. It was inevitable that, whilst he had hold of me, we were going to kiss again. He pressed me up against the side of the car. We kissed and held each other very close. I could feel his manhood pressing up against me. He was excited, and so was I.

'I think we are on first names now, don't you?' he said, laughing.

'Yes, I think so,' I replied, and we both laughed.

'Thomas,' he said.

'Catherine,' I said, and we both laughed again.

We held each other close as he helped me up the steps to

the entrance hall. We walked across the entrance hall to the other side of the room. A door opened into a very large dining area that surrounded a dance floor and a stage area. A band was playing. As he walked me over to a table, I noticed that all the women were dressed in eveningwear. I was quite under dressed, so I immediately felt insecure and out of place.

Ours was a large oval table that seated at least ten persons. There were only two remaining seats. Thomas took me to one and introduced the persons at the table. I could not remember all of their names, but I did remember some. He took the last seat, which was situated opposite mine.

When we were settled, Thomas looked across at me and asked if I was okay. I mentioned quietly that I was not hungry, so I was only interested in a starter. He said he would order for me, something light and easy to eat. I nodded my approval. When the waiter asked what I was to drink, I whispered that I would like some fruit juice in sparkling water in a large wine glass. It would look as if I was drinking alcohol, but I wouldn't be.

Then, the questions from the table started. Someone asked, 'How long have you known Thomas?'

'Quite a while,' I replied.

'How long are you here for?'

'A few weeks or so.'

'What do you do for a living?'

'I run my own haulage business.'

Before any more questions came my way, I said, 'I must apologize to the table, but Thomas did not tell me there would be a dress code tonight, and as a result, I feel wrongly dressed.'

'I bet Thomas is in the doghouse now,' said one of the guests.

'He is a dead man walking,' I said, and most of the people at the table laughed. So did Thomas.

'Come dance with me,' Thomas said as he helped me out of my seat.

We just held each other close on the dance floor. Neither of us spoke. We just enjoyed the feel of each other.

'The food is here,' Thomas said, so we made our way back to our seats.

I did manage to eat some of the starter. I let Thomas know that I would like to go to the restrooms. He dutifully came and helped me out of my seat.

On my way to the restrooms, I asked a waiter to come with me. I borrowed his pad and pen, wrote a note to Thomas, and instructed the waiter to give him the note after I had left. I planned to take a taxi as I had seen some at the entrance to the golf club.

When I asked the waiter to give the note to the gentleman at our table, I explained he was a judge. 'Do you know who you are giving the note to?' I asked.

He replied, 'Yes, I know who you refer to. It is Judge Thomas Hague. He owns this golf club and spa.' I was genuinely surprised.

My note read, 'Thank you, Thomas. I am in your debt. I am fine now, and I know what to do to help my son. Please apologize to the table for my leaving so abruptly. From your English woman with attitude. Love, Catherine. X'

***

I was relieved to be back at my hotel, and I collected my envelope from reception. In my basement room, I read through all the paperwork that Thomas had given to me. I wanted to make sure that I was familiar with all his instructions.

A knock came on my door. With no peephole in my door, there was no way I was going to answer it.

'Catherine, open the door. It's Thomas,' said Thomas Hague.

I opened the door to him, and he entered, the door closing behind him, self-locking. 'I was worried about you, so I had to come to make sure you were all right.'

I sat back down at the table and said, 'I promise you that I am fine now. Thanks to you, I can move on with purpose. I know exactly what I have to do to help my son. I shall always be in your debt.'

Thomas sat on the side of the bed. A deafening silence came into the room. It was Thomas who broke the silence when he said, 'Catherine, can I share your bed with you for a couple of hours or so? I intend to fuck you.'

Those words made me jump; in fact, they excited me.

'Sorry, no.' I began to stammer. 'I cannot … er … no, Thomas, I cannot … er … I have not been with a man for many years … um … my husband and I are not intimate … I will let you down … will not know what to do with you … um … I do not know how to react with you … it will be disastrous … er …' I gave up trying to explain myself.

The silence returned.

Thomas repeated, 'Catherine, can I share your bed with you for a couple of hours or so? I intend to fuck you. You do not have to do anything. I will not hurt you. I will not let you down; therefore, you will not let me down. Now come here!'

The only thing that was in my head at that moment was that life is full of missed opportunities, and this opportunity, I did not want to miss. I walked over to him.

As he sat on the side of the bed, he stood me between his legs. We did not speak; we just looked into each other's eyes. He removed my dress, and as it fell to the floor, I kicked it away. I wore only a silk slip under my dress. I did not wear a bra. Thomas ran his hands up and down my slip, pausing to hold my breasts. He ran his hands up my stockings as far as my knickers, which he pulled down to the floor. I kicked them away. As he stood up, he lifted my slip above my head and let it fell to the floor. I kicked my slip away.

'I think I shall leave the stockings and suspenders. I find them exciting,' whispered Thomas. 'Lie on the bed for me.'

Thomas took his clothes off. I could see his penis; it was erect and throbbing. He lay on my right arm, his left arm under my head, holding my left arm. I could not move. He kissed me repeatedly, from soft, seductive kisses to hard, urgent, demanding kisses, whilst all the time stroking my body with his right hand. I felt him stroking my breasts, squeezing my nipples hard, stroking my stomach, stroking my groin area, and then between my legs, making sure he gently stroked my clitoris. As he rolled over onto me, he released both my arms. I put my arms around his shoulders and pulled him towards me at the same time I felt his penetration. My desire for him became erotic pleasure. I knew I was going to climax very soon. Thomas whispered, 'Not yet, Catherine, not yet.' Soon I was climaxing, and I felt Thomas ejaculate. I had the most tremendous orgasm. I had never experienced anything like that before.

We lay in each other's arms, holding one another so tightly. A feeling of love for this man came to me. A love that felt so strong. I wanted this feeling of love for Thomas to stay with me forever and a day.

Soon, Thomas was dressed and ready to leave. I buried my head in the pillow as I did not want to see him go.

'Take care,' he said. 'Tomorrow, you have a long day ahead of you. If you ever come to visit your son, let me know when and where you will be staying. I really want to see you again.' He continued, 'Catherine, you did not let me down.' The door opened, closed, and self-locked. I was on my own again.

***

I was up bright and early. I checked out of the hotel, put all my belongings into my hire car, and made my way to the lawyer's office.

The receptionist showed me into Mr. Stephen Hewell's office. After listening to my account of the circumstances that led me to ask him for his services, he took the money orders from me along with Tony's passport. 'Rest assured, Mrs. Riding, I will act on your son's instructions, and I will advise him on what needs to be done. I shall visit him this afternoon to introduce myself and to ask him for his version of events on that fateful night. I will let him know that he can contact me twenty-four seven.'

I asked Mr. Hewell to keep me informed, by phone or by fax, of everything that concerned my son. He agreed. We exchanged contact details, and I left feeling quite optimistic.

Back in the hire car, I reset the sat nav and set off to find the British Consulate. I had plenty of time, so I started to relax a little.

My thoughts recalled holding Thomas in my arms after such a wonderful love making session. I felt a thrill racing all through my body. *Oh, how I loved that man.* I wondered if I would ever hold him in my arms again.

Before long, I reached my destination. I was in front of the offices of the British Consulate. I could see the Holiday Inn

Hotel next door. I had plenty of time before my appointment, so I booked into the hotel, rested up, and refreshed myself.

When it was my appointment time, I walked to the Consulate. I asked to see Mrs. Margaret Hayes. I had to talk to her through a glass partition. With a large picture of our queen looking down on me, I asked her for help because my son was being held in the Miami-Dade County detention center. Her attitude was that my son was in the American judicial system and that there was nothing she could do to help him. I insisted that she arrange for a telephone call with my son – immediately, I insisted. I also insisted that she keep watch over my son, making sure he was safe and in good health. I would be phoning the Consulate on a weekly basis and expected a report about the well-being of my son, Tony.

I was taken beyond the glass partition and into a light, warm office. I saw a phone on the desk. Fifteen minutes later, a call came from the detention center. Tony was there, at the other end of the phone.

I had to be so strong and positive whilst I was talking to him. He was emotional and crying. He asked me to raise the one hundred thousand dollars for his bail. I reassured him that the lawyer and the British Consulate would be doing everything in their power to make sure that justice was done. I asked him to be strong, and I promised him that I would be back out to visit him once I found out when his hearing was. The phone line went dead. Then, I cried and cried. I felt so heartbroken. I could do nothing to help him.

I left all my contact details and the contact details of the lawyer with Mrs. Hayes, and then I left.

Back in my hotel room, I contacted my airline and booked my return flight home. Eleven o'clock in the morning was my flight time. I contacted my husband to let him know what time I would land back in England.

Exhausted, I fell into a nervous sleep.

I was awakened by the room phone ringing. There was only one person who knew I was there, so I answered, 'Hello, you.'

Thomas laughed. 'Well, tell me how you got on today,' he said with such a lovely, soft voice.

I gave him a summary of what had happened. 'Have you managed to book your return flight?' he asked.

'Yes, I have.'

'Give me the details of your flight.'

This I did, then silence. 'Thomas,' I said.

'Yes?'

'Put your arms around me.'

'They are around you.'

'Hold me tight.'

'I am holding you very tight.'

'Goodbye,' I said, and I put the phone receiver down. Only then did I break down and cry.

***

The next morning, I was at the airport in good time. As I checked in, I was told that I had been upgraded to first class, which is now business class. I knew who had done that, and the air hostess confirmed the same. I owed him so much, and I would never be able to repay him. My beautiful Judge Thomas Hague.

Before I went through to the departure lounge, I found a newsagent. I bought a lovely card that showed two cartoon people— a little boy and a little girl— waving goodbye to each other. The little girl had a tear in her eye. I wrote in the card, 'I have just checked in at the airport. It was a lovely gesture to upgrade my ticket. Think of me often, kindly, and lovingly. Never forget, your Catherine.'

I found Thomas' address on the papers he had given to me, and after writing it on the envelope, I posted the card.

I then made my way through to the departure lounge.

Chapter 3
Back Home

My husband, Richard, was so pleased to have me safely back home. I was relieved to be back home with at least some structure for the care of my son Tony.

I sat for hours talking to my husband, telling him about everything that had happened after he and the girls had left for England. The only part I did not tell him about was Thomas Hague seducing me and fucking me. I did not feel any guilt about that and the fact that I had been unfaithful to Richard.

Richard's cancer had not improved, and the radiotherapy had not had any effect. If he was well enough, he was due to start chemotherapy the following week.

Back at my desk at work, I thought about Thomas. It all seemed like a dream, but it was very true.

Every day at work, I wrote a letter to Tony, posting it on my way home. I waited and waited for some news – any news – about what was to happen to Tony. I telephone the British Consulate a couple of times, and they had not heard anything.

Then, at last, one morning, I arrived at work to find a fax from Stephen Hewell, the lawyer. The results of the medical examination of the young woman showed no sexual activity on or around that night. It did show that she was sexually active. A first hearing had been arranged at the court, and the young woman in question had failed to appear. Mr. Hewell had instructed my son to accept a plea bargain. He was to be taken to the courthouse and charged with sexual battery. He was to plead guilty and would then be sentenced to 364 days in jail. He would probably serve a sentence of maybe ten months, followed by deportation back to England. He concluded that he would contact me again when all of this had been completed.

The nightmare was nearly over! I felt as if a great weight had been lifted from my soul. I returned a fax to Mr. Hewell, thanking him for his advice and his services. I immediately returned home to tell the family the good news.

'You must visit Tony as soon as possible,' said Richard. 'He must be so relieved to know what the future is going to be for him. I shall book your flights, and I shall book you into a better hotel this time. I shall phone the Consulate, tell them of our news, and instruct them to arrange a visiting order for you.'

Richard arranged the flights for the first week in October. I would have four days in Miami before my return flight. A visiting order was arranged for my second day there. I was so excited.

What was I to do about Thomas? I really wanted to see him again – to hold him, to feel him, to love him, and to have sex with him again.

The next time I was at work, I sent a fax to Judge Thomas Hague. I gave him the times and details of my flights and the name and address of the hotel I would be staying at. I also told him about the accepted plea bargain.

I could not wait to see Tony. The whole experience had been an absolute nightmare. I knew now that I could relax in the knowledge that he would be home soon enough. As for my wanting to see the judge … *well, that would be up to him.* The thought of him holding me sent shivers all over my body. I lived in hope that he would try to see me while I was in Miami.

Chapter 4
First Visit

At last, I was back in Miami. I made my way by taxi from the airport to the hotel that Richard had booked for me. It was a beautiful hotel, right on the sea front near the boardwalk.

I had not hired a car this time. It seemed much easier to use taxis for all of my journeys.

I had treated myself to a complete new wardrobe. Perhaps I would see the judge again, so I wanted to look my best, and my clothing had to suit any venue he might take me to. I unpacked, made myself a coffee, and relaxed in the comfort of the beautiful hotel room.

The following day, I prepared to visit Tony in the afternoon. I booked a taxi, and before long, I was at the jail, waiting to be admitted to the visiting suite.

I was so surprised when I saw him. He had grown a large beard. He was more of a man than a boy. He was so confident in the way he acted and talked. He had met so many interesting people, and he had made many new friends. We held each other for a while.

'Don't worry about me, Mum. I have met a wonderful preacher who comes from Costa Rica,' said Tony. He continued, 'I am hoping to visit him when I am released from here. Obviously, I will come home first, but I intend to travel and live life to the fullest.' We both laughed, but he did have a good point. *Why not travel and live life to the fullest?*

That night, back in my hotel room, I wondered why Thomas had not contacted me. Perhaps he had not received my fax, or perhaps he did not want to see me.

The following day, I relaxed by the pool. I thought I would look better with a tan. That night, I curled up by the television with all the windows open letting the sea breeze blow past me.

A knock came at the door. Looking through the peephole, I could see that it was Thomas Hague. I opened the door, said, 'Hello, you,' and I let him in. As my door closed, Thomas put his arms around me and kissed me like there was no tomorrow. He talked through our kissing. 'I have missed you … I have thought of you so many times.'

'I have missed you and thought about you so many times. I have so looked forward to seeing you and holding you. I didn't know if you were coming to see me or not,' I said whilst holding him so tight and kissing him back.

'Let me see your airline tickets,' said Thomas.

I showed him my tickets, and I was so surprise by his reaction. 'These are totally unacceptable!' Thomas said. 'If we are to have any sort of a relationship, four days every few months is totally unacceptable. Phone the airline now and make your return flight in three weeks' time.'

I hesitated at first. I was thinking about my husband and the business back home.

'Tell your husband that you have met people who live and work out here, and they have invited you to stay with them for longer than the four days you had. Tell him that a four-day turnaround is not going to do you any good. You feel exhausted. You really fancy staying and having a good holiday-type break, maybe seeing Tony one more time.' He continued, 'Give me your airline tickets, and I will change your return booking. Maybe an extra three weeks would be great.'

I gave him the airline tickets, and I let him do what he wanted to do. I then phoned Richard and said exactly what Thomas had suggested. To my surprise, Richard agreed and said it made more sense, and it would do me good to slow down and relax for a change. With that said and all done, Thomas and I fell into each other's arms.

We kissed and kissed and held each other so close. 'Come, let us go and walk the boardwalk. We can find a good eating place along there. A few drinks will do us both good,' said Thomas, and we both laughed.

As we walked along the sea front, I wrapped myself around his arm. It was magical – all the little lights twinkling around each beach bar, the feel of the sea breeze, the smell of all the different foods on offer. All this was interrupted by a woman confronting Thomas. 'So this is why you have not called me this week!' she shouted.

'Susan, this is Catherine from England. Catherine, this is Susan, a very, very close friend of mine.'

Susan walked away, shouting, 'That is it! I have had enough!' And she stormed off.

Thomas carried on as normal. He did not mention Susan again, so I did not.

When we returned to my room, Thomas said that we would be leaving for his place in the Keys the following morning.

'We shall have a holiday,' he said as he took all my clothes off and removed his as well.

Between the sheets on my bed, we kissed, we stroked, licked, and kissed every part of each other's bodies. As Thomas lay down, I sat across him, easing his penis inside of me. He held me so he could manoeuvre me. The desire I had for him turned into pure pleasure as Thomas moved me whilst holding both my breasts. It was not long before we both came. Again, I had never experienced anything like it. It was so fantastic. *Wow. How I loved that man!*

***

The following morning, all ready and packed, I checked out of the hotel, and Thomas and I drove to his house.

'I only have an hour's work to do,' he said. 'I shall get Annie to make us some breakfast and pack me a bag.'

We arrived at his house. It was huge—a mansion-type house. I could see a swimming pool beyond the house and tennis courts. All the grounds were landscaped to perfection.

He helped me out of the car and helped me up the stone steps to the house. Using the side entrance door, which was a stable door with the bottom half closed, he walked me into a large living kitchen. 'Sit there and don't move,' he said, 'and I will go and find Annie.' With that, he left the room.

On his return, he was with a beautiful woman who was a lot older than he. She was tall, slim, and smartly dressed. She had dark, reddish-brown short hair and beautiful blue eyes.

'Annie, this is Catherine,' Thomas said. 'Catherine, this is Annie. Annie is not just my housekeeper. She is my own PA – personal assistant – at home. I could not function without her, but much more than that, she is my best friend and saviour.'

'Make us some breakfast, please, whilst I finish some work off,' he said to Annie, and then he disappeared through a pair of large wood-and-glass doors.

I heard a car pull up outside and a woman shouting, 'Thomas! Are you there? Are you coming out to play?' Good grief, I thought to myself, *How many women does Thomas have on the go at one time?*

I went outside and showed myself. I recognized the woman. She had been at the table at the country club the first night I had gone out with Thomas.

'Hello, Janet. It is Janet, isn't it?' I said smugly.

'Oh, yes, Catherine. Hello. I didn't know you were here staying with Thomas,' Janet said.

'Yes,' I said, mocking her. 'I am sorry, but Thomas is busy at the moment and does not want to be disturbed. What did you want Thomas to play?'

'Er … er … Tennis! If he was free, that is,' Janet replied, and she started her engine and drove away.

It was obvious that Annie did not like Janet, as I saw her smiling at me sideways when I returned to the kitchen.

After breakfast, Thomas disappeared again through the large wood-and-glass doors. He told me to look around if I wanted to.

I was really fascinated to have a good look around the house. I could see most of the grounds, so it was the inside of the house that appealed to me.

The house had ten bedrooms, all with en suites. Each one was colour coordinated. The pink room was obviously used by a woman. There were clothes in the wardrobe, perfume and make-up on the dressing table, cuddly toys on the bed.

I walked up to the next level. I could see Thomas at his

desk, talking on the phone. I wandered in, even though Thomas had tried to dismiss me. I had a good look around the room, and then, walking behind Thomas, I kissed him on his neck, rubbed my small breasts in his face, and ruffled his hair, all whilst he was trying to have a serious phone conversation.

When he had finished his phone call, he literally dragged me to his bedroom. It was, to be polite, a man cave. One thing I did notice that stopped me in my tracks was a cartoon of a little girl and a little boy waving goodbye to one another. It was my card – the one I had sent to him some months ago. He'd had it framed. I was really touched! Perhaps Thomas loved me as much as I loved him … but words cannot explain how much.

'I have never had a woman in this bed,' said Thomas, laughing all the time as he chased me around the room.

'Perhaps they didn't want to come into this room,' I said, laughing back at him.

What followed was a sex session with me on my side, Thomas behind me. He really did make love to me that way, very gently entering my vagina from behind … *fantastic.* He kept one hand on my breasts and the other hand between my legs.

'I want to remember this, for when I am having solo sex,' he said, quite seriously. 'Please leave me alone now. I really have to finish some work before we can go. Have a shower and get ready. I want to leave within the hour,' he said quite sternly.

When I returned to the kitchen, I asked Annie about the pink bedroom. She said it belonged to a woman called Susan. I'd thought as much.

***

We arrived at Thomas' holiday home in the Keys. He showed me a large yacht that he owned. It was moored in the harbour nearby. The property was a good-sized, three-bedroom bungalow. It did not take us long to make ourselves comfortable for the best-ever holiday I had ever had.

Every day was different – from walking the sea front to sailing on his boat. Most of the time, we rested in the sun. Thomas would put his glasses on and read for hours. We could go for hours and not say a single word to each other. We felt so comfortable in each other's company.

The nights were wonderful – pretty bars, good food, plenty of drink, lively music, and dancing. Thomas knew so many people there. They were all his friends, and they became my friends as the weeks went by.

A trip one day to Key West resulted in a visit to a jewellery store. Thomas jokingly asked me if I wanted a ring. I did not answer him. He just laughed and said he was going to buy me two. He bought me a beautiful pair of large diamond earrings.

Every night, we loved each other and slept wrapped in each other's arms.

All too soon, it was time for us to leave. Thomas was to take me directly to the airport for my flight home.

All the way to the airport, not a word was spoken. When we parked at the departure car park, all Thomas said was that, when I next came to visit, he wanted me to stay with him so I should not book a hotel. 'Three weeks,' he demanded. With that, he drove to the entrance of the departures where airport staff helped me with my luggage. When I turned around, Thomas had gone.

As usual, Thomas had upgraded me to first class. All the way home, I felt so lost and upset. I knew I did not need to worry too much about Tony. Tony seemed so positive, which made me relax a little. I just knew that I was going to miss my Judge Thomas Hague so much. How I loved that man!

Chapter 5
Returning to Normality

This time, when I returned home, everything seemed different. Richard was so pleased to have me back home. I think he knew what had been happening to me over in America. He did not ask any questions, so I did not have to answer them. He commented on my lovely earrings, but never once did he ask where they had come from.

Work was just the same. Every day, I wrote to Tony and posted the letter on my way home. The girls, Carol and Jennifer, were getting on with their lives. Carol was away at university, and by all accounts, she had found a really lovely boy to settle down with. Jennifer was heading that way too. Having achieved her grades, she was now on her way to choosing her university.

Richard's health was becoming a major problem. We needed oxygen at home; chemo had not done any good. He had so many different health issues, and it was hard to predict which health issue required the most help.

I felt lonely inside. I was so fed up with my life. I missed Thomas with every part of my body and soul.

I worked out that Tony would probably be released at the end of May, and that meant that I probably would have only one last visit to Miami. I decided that a visit to Tony around the end of January would work out well for Tony and for me.

'I would like to visit Tony, maybe one last time, about the end of January,' I said to Richard. 'What do you think?'

'I personally don't think you need to visit him again, but if it makes you feel better about the situation, by all means, I will book your flights and accommodation.'

'Yes, I think I will go. I need only flights, as I have some good friends out there who want me to stay with them.' I continued, 'I will book the flights, and maybe I shall stay for three weeks or so as it will be my last visit over there.'

I watched my husband's reaction to that statement. I knew that he knew what was happening. He never asked any questions, and again, I did not have to answer any.

Once my flight was booked, I faxed the details to Thomas. I wrote a note and asked him to confirm that he had received the flight information, which he did. It was all so formal, but who knows who had access to the faxes?

I was so excited about this coming trip. I was excited at seeing Tony again, and I was excited at being with Thomas again. I could not wait.

Chapter 6
Second Visit

At last, it was time for me to fly out to Miami. I had a suitcase full of new beautiful clothes, new make-up, and new shoes. I had never been so excited about a trip.

I fell asleep on the plane, and before long, we were landing at Miami airport. As I exited the departure gates, I saw a man holding a board with my name on it. One of Thomas's drivers had been sent to collect me.

As we pulled up at Thomas's house, I could see that there was a party in full swing. People were gathered in the grounds and in the house. The driver left my case at the bottom of the stone steps and said he would later take it to my room when he knew which room I was going to be given. *Ouch!* I thought. I made my way up the steps and into the kitchen. It was quiet in there. I looked out over the grounds. There were people dancing, drinking, eating, and generally enjoying themselves. The music was very loud, and as I looked at the makeshift dance floor, I saw Thomas dancing with Susan. They were very close. In fact, I thought Thomas was kissing her cheek. I felt physically sick.

I stayed in the kitchen for a little while. The driver must have told Thomas that I had arrived because it was not long before he came running into the kitchen.

Holding me tight and talking through his kisses, he said, 'I have been waiting for weeks to do this. What are you doing in here alone?'

'Sorry. I saw you and Susan dancing, and I felt very uncomfortable. I needed to gather my thoughts,' I replied.

'Susan is with me for many weeks, while you are with me for only three weeks every few months. What do you expect?' he said, looking very annoyed with me.

'You are right. I was a little jealous. Come here and hold me. I have been looking forward to seeing you for months. Nothing is going to spoil my visit to you.' We both laughed and held each other tight.

I joined in with the other guests, and it was a great night. Well, before everyone had left, Thomas grabbed a bottle of brandy, two glasses, and took me to his bedroom. My suitcase had been delivered to his room, thank goodness.

'Please tell me that Susan is not stopping the night,' I said.

'No, she is not,' replied Thomas.

We spent one fantastic night of desire, sex, pleasure, and love. We were so fantastic together in bed. We slept together, wrapped in each other's arms.

The next morning at breakfast, Thomas brought me a gift. I opened the gift bag, and inside was a ring case. I opened it, and sure enough, there was a beautiful square diamond ring.

'Put it on your engagement finger,' demanded Thomas. I had always removed my wedding ring when I was going to be with Thomas, so I put the diamond ring on. It looked so good, and I was so thrilled with it. What it represented, I had no idea, but it felt good and correct.

'Thomas, this ring is beautiful. Does this ring mean that you are in love with me?' I said coyly.

'It means that I love you as much as you love me, and we both know that is a hell of a lot.' We hugged each other, kissing and laughing, even though we had no future to look forward to.

'I have to work some days, so you will have to occupy your-self,' he told me. 'Annie will take you shopping if you want,' said Thomas.

'That is fine by me,' I said.

'Next week, we will be flying to LA. We have been invited to my parents' golden wedding celebrations at the Golf Resort Hotel and Spa at Santa Barbara.'

'Sounds great. Will I be meeting your family?' I asked.

'Of course,' Thomas said. 'You are my fiancée, are you not?'

'Now I am nervous, Thomas,' I said quietly.

***

The day arrived for us to fly to LA. We would be there in a couple of hours. The Hague Corporation, of which Thomas was a part, developed many golf resorts all over America. Thomas was in partnership with his older brother, Justin.

We were shown to our suite. It was magnificent. That afternoon, Thomas introduced me to all his family members. His parents were charming. His brother, Justin, and his wife and children were also charming.

Thomas and I avoided all questions about us getting married and settling down. He told everyone we were still practising, whatever that meant. His present to his parents on their special day was a cruise to the fiords in Norway.

Thomas had very little to do with the Hague Corporation. He was concentrating on his ambition of being elected to the senate. That was a long time off, and being a county court judge was just a stepping stone. Next stop would be Florida state supreme court justice.

The rest of the afternoon, we toured around the resort.

The evening activities were to include a five-course dinner, followed by entertainment, music, and dancing. All this was to be held in a huge hall.

Thomas looked so handsome in his dinner suit, and I looked like a million dollars in my evening dress. We made a lovely couple. I think all of his family could see that we were in love.

That evening, while we were having pre-meal drinks, I noticed a party of about six men, all dressed in Scottish kilts – the full highland wear. They looked superb. They were surrounded by women. I must admit that they did look the part. I wondered if they were part of the evening entertainment.

As I was looking at them across the dance floor, one of them really caught my eye. He was tall, well built, had blond curly hair, and his eyes looked as if they were a bright blue. I could not help staring at him. His kilt, the tartan, and sporran all added to my fascination. All of a sudden, he was staring back at me. Our eyes fixed on each other's. I felt a rush of sexual thrills all through my body. I was so embarrassed, and I bushed. How could I feel that for anyone else except for Thomas?

We were shown to our table, and the meal was served. After the meal, the tables were removed, and the evening entertainment was about to begin. The party of Scotsmen was brought to our table by Justin, who introduced them as Squire Donald McFadden, laird of the Thistle Isles and his party. Squire Donald McFadden had sold a considerable amount of land to the Hague Corporation for the development of a golf resort in Scotland, and I had thought he was the evening's entertainment!

'May I dance with your fiancée?' Donald McFadden asked Thomas.

'If she wishes,' said Thomas.

Donald McFadden held my hand and led me onto the dance floor. He looked magnificent in his kilt and jacket.

He held me tight as we danced and whispered, 'That is my sporran you can feel … Catherine, isn't it?'

'Funny!' I replied, and we both laughed. 'Yes, Catherine it is, Donald.'

As we talked, I was looking into those fantastic bright blue eyes. He was exciting me, and I was embarrassed by the whole episode.

'Where in England are you from?' asked Donald McFadden.

'Not far from Lancaster, so not that far from the Scottish border,' I told him.

'Do you ride?'

'I used to do when I was younger.'

'I will give you my card, and if you ever feel like contacting me, I shall show you my stables and perhaps give you a refresher riding lesson. My stables are just outside Lancaster, so you have no excuse not to come and visit me. What do you think?' asked Donald.

He was holding me so close and looking straight into my eyes. I could feel my heart beating. I could feel the sexual attraction between us. 'Yes, I think I will contact you. You had better choose a very docile horse for me if you ever think that I would be prepared to try riding a horse again,' I said, and we both laughed.

I returned to Thomas at the table. I felt flushed and embarrassed. I just wanted Donald to disappear. He was surrounded by women, so I knew he would not bother me. Or so I thought!

Later, as I left the restroom, Donald was waiting for me.

'I have something in my sporran for you. Do you want to put your hand in it and see what it is?' said Donald, knowing he was making me blush.

'Behave yourself, Donald. I am not going to put my hand in there. Something might bite me!' I answered. We both laughed again.

Donald retrieved his business card from the sporran. 'Keep this safe. I really want you to contact me when you are back home.' With that said, he returned to his party.

I did not see Donald after that. I was so relieved that we were to prepare to go home the following day. The flight was at lunchtime, and we were back home by early evening, in time to eat whatever Annie had prepared for us, followed by a walk in the grounds, sex, and cuddles in bed.

I spent the rest of my time there enjoying the company of Thomas. I so loved that man. We had many meals out with his friends and colleagues. On the days when he was not presiding at court, we would visit places of interest, go for long walks, or sit and read by the pool. These were just a few things that occupied our days, but the nights were ours and for enjoying each other's bodies. Sex was wonderful. We never tired of it and never had any problems. We always slept wrapped in each other's arms.

A few days before I was due to fly home, Thomas was not presiding at court until the afternoon session, so we decided to have a leisurely breakfast together.

All of a sudden, Thomas turned to me and said, 'Leave your husband and come and live with me. We can start a life together as it should be.'

'I cannot leave Richard. He needs me at the moment.'

'You can leave him. I will help in any way that I can.'

'Sorry, Thomas, no, I can't leave him.'

'I am asking you again. Leave your husband and come and live with me.'

I took a deep breath and slowly said, 'No, I will not leave my husband.'

'Then pack your bags and leave now. I never want to hear from you or see you again. When I return home tonight, I do not want you here. I want you long gone. Do I make myself clear?' He went out to his car and drove away.

I was so shocked. I knew that I had chosen my husband

and that Thomas and I were now over. I did not cry. I packed all my belongings and asked Annie to order me a taxi. Annie was more upset than I was, as she did not know what was happening. I put my ring back into its box and placed it on Thomas's desk. I wrote all my contact details in Thomas' diary. With all that done, I hugged and kissed Annie, got into my taxi, and drove away.

I went straight to the airport. I did not bother trying to see Tony, as he'd told me he was not bothered about my not visiting him. The airline had a spare seat on the early-morning flight, so I booked into the airport hotel and waited there. I had never felt as lonely as I did then, and I cried. I boarded that early-morning flight knowing that I would never see Thomas again. I was a broken woman.

Chapter 7
Home Again

Life went back to normal. A few months later, Tony was on his way home after being deported from America. We had one short phone call from Mrs. Hayes at the British Consulate telling us that Tony had been put on a plane for England. She had no idea which plane or which airport it was heading to.

We made an educated guess that the airport would be Heathrow, and Richard and I drove as quickly as we could in order to be there to greet him.

We had been right, and we both found it very emotional to see him walk through the arrivals gate. He seemed so grown up – not the young boy we had taken on holiday.

When we were home, Tony went upstairs to his room to unpack and presumably get all his thoughts in order. It was a dramatic time for him.

I had my family back, but the girls had flown my nest, and Tony was talking about travelling, so he would soon fly as well.

Later that evening, Tony gave me a present. It was small and wrapped in multi-coloured gift paper. 'It is not from me,' Tony said. 'It's from that judge.'

My blood ran cold … I knew what was wrapped in the paper.

'Open it,' said Richard.

I slowly took the wrapping paper off. There in front of me was the ring case. I opened the box, and there it was – the beautiful engagement ring that Thomas had given me.

'This Thomas and Annie you have talked about must think an awful lot of you to go and buy you such an expensive ring,' said Richard.

I could tell that Richard knew about Thomas, but he never once insisted about any explanations. I put the ring away.

Richard's health was not good. He was getting worse by the day. He was always cheerful. He never asked about my times in Miami, and I never told him.

I was back in the old routine. I would sit at my desk at work and worry about Richard. What would happen when I could no longer look after him? Caring for him now had become hard work – making sure he was taking the correct medication, bathing him, making food that he could digest easily, and trying to keep him occupied. I asked my doctor if he had any idea how long before Richard would die. I knew it was only months, but it had been only months over twelve months ago. The doctor could give me no idea as to when. I did not want Richard to die, but I knew that it was going to happen, and I needed to know when.

It was about time that I started taking some of the responsibility for our future. I had to stop fretting over Thomas. I made some decisions, and when I returned home one evening, I said to Richard, 'I am going to sell the haulage business.'

'Why?' asked Richard.

'Because I am bloody well fed up with it, and I want you and me to have more time together and some more money in the bank. We will be able to afford anything we want.'

'What about your future when I am no longer here?' Richard said quietly.

'To hell with my future when you are no longer here. It is the here and now that I want to enjoy,' I shouted.

***

The next day I contacted our accountants and gave them instructions to finalize the business accounts and put the whole of the business – land and buildings – all up for sale. Obviously, I had to keep the business running as normal whilst it was up for sale, but I had no problem with that. As for how much we could ask for the business, well, it was all open to negotiation.

Our accountant placed a figure on the worth of it all. Richard and I were pleasantly surprised at the first valuation. We knew that anyone interested in our business would in all probability close the business down, keeping only the assets, especially the wagons and the customer debtors list. The land and buildings would probably go for planning, maybe housing. Our drivers would probably lose their jobs, but I had made a decision, and I intended to get rid of the business.

It took quite a few months before we finally walked away with a considerable amount of money. I could spend more time doing things with Richard.

We took quite a few escorted coach holidays, mainly to Scotland. On one such trip, we drove past signposts pointing to the Thistle Isles and surrounding low lands. That must have been Squire Donald McFadden's land. I recalled my meeting with Donald, and I smiled to myself. What a wonderful time I'd had in America.

For the next twelve months, Richard and I travelled, entertained family and friends, and generally lived life to the fullest. Then, one day, Richard said that he was feeling unwell. He had all the symptoms of a bad case of flu. I made sure the doctor came to see him, and I was surprised when the doctor insisted that my husband was to be admitted to hospital. An ambulance came, and Richard was admitted to ward sixteen. He was having problems with his breathing and was placed on oxygen. They told me that he had pneumonia and that there would be nothing to worry about as he was on large doses of antibiotics and would soon be feeling much better. I returned home that night so relieved. In the early morning, however, I received that dreadful phone call from the hospital. They wanted me to go to the hospital as Richard had taken a turn for the worse.

I rushed back to the hospital, and as I entered the ward where Richard was, I knew that I was too late. Richard had passed away a few minutes before I arrived there.

****

My Tony, Carol, and Jennifer all returned home for the funeral. The day of the funeral went according to plan. The weather was good, the service was good, and the internment was over with in no time. Many people came to pay their respects. I was just acting on autopilot. That night, I curled up with my son and daughters. My life had just changed forever.

Within days, Tony, Carol, and Jennifer had left to resume their own lives.

I was left all on my own in a large house. I had money in the bank and little else. I kept myself occupied by decorating some of the rooms and landscaping the huge garden. I was lonely. I did not feel that I had a purpose in life. I really did feel sorry for myself.

A few months after my husband's death, I decided that I was no longer going to rattle around in our house. I was going to sell up and downsize.

At least I had plenty to occupy myself with. From car boots to charity shops, I spent most of my time clearing away items that were no longer of no use to me. It was like erasing years of my life. Before long, I had an offer on the house, and I decided to accept. I then started my search for a new house, or as I wanted to think of it, a new home.

A few months later, I had moved into a beautiful two-bedroom detached bungalow. It was a few miles away from the large family house, but it was in a rural area with fields and woods to walk in.

I was pleasantly surprised at how beautiful each room was, even the conservatory. The gardens were considerably smaller than I was used to, but it was easier for me to maintain.

There had been so many changes in my life, but one thing had not changed. I was lonely. So lonely. I knew I had to get on with my life, and I was the only one who could change things for the better.

One night, I phoned Thomas's home telephone number. Why, I did not know. I just wanted to hear his voice and tell him about Richard's death.

When someone answered, I said, 'Could I possibly speak to Judge Thomas Hague, please?'

'Sorry,' the person who answered said, 'There is no Judge Hague at this address." I then realised that my beautiful Judge Thomas Hague must have moved residency.

The next day, I was so determined to find out where Thomas was that I phoned his chambers. I had no luck there. I was just told that he no longer presided in that area and had moved to Los Angeles. 'Do you have a forwarding telephone number? Do you know where he moved to?' The person I was talking to was not prepared to divulge any more information, but he did say that the judge was away on holiday with his wife for a month or so before he took up his new position with the Hague Corporation. The telephone line had gone dead. Whoever had answered my call was not prepared to answer any more of my questions.

I was shocked! Of course, people get on with their lives, and changes do happen, but I was shocked. I never thought I would lose contact with the love of my life.

From that day, my attitude changed. I looked at myself in the mirror and immediately made an appointment at the hairdressers. I threw out all my old clothes and spent days buying new, modern clothes.

I joined the golf club that offered a gym, a swimming pool, organized activities for my age group, and social evening events from dinner dances to big band nights.

I was soon accepted and made plenty friends; some of them even became very good close friends. My social diary was filling up, and my loneliness was becoming bearable, but that did not stop me from fretting over Thomas Hague. He was never far from my thoughts.

It was not long before I was elected onto the golf club's committee. I was looking better, and I was proud of the way I looked. I considered myself quite attractive, and although men were interested in me, I never accepted any unwanted attentions.

I occasionally went on dates, but I always made it clear that I was not looking for a relationship. Friends, yes … lovers, no.

The golf club was undergoing some drastic changes. There had been a new owner, who had accumulated 54 percent of the club's shares, although we had yet to meet him. Plans had been drawn up, approved, and passed for a large extension. The golf club was to become a golf resort with a spa. It would also accommodate a large suite for social events, discos, dances, even wedding receptions, and the like.

The committee members were to remain, and they would help in the organization of all social events, charitable events, and fund-raising events. This pleased me, as I thoroughly enjoyed the hustle and bustle of arranging any event.

One such event was a big band night. A band, singers, dancing, competitions, and, of course, a large half-time buffet were planned. All had been arranged, and on the afternoon prior to the event, I was there with other committee members to take delivery of some of the buffet food. I was standing at the bar when my closest friends, Sarah and Judith, arrived. We all ordered coffee and settled down to have a good chat.

'I have met the new owner,' said Sarah, 'and what a handsome fellow he is!'

'Is he married?' asked Judith. She was never interested unless they were single and available.

We laughed at her, and Sarah replied, 'No. He's just your type – single and free!' We all laughed again.

'There he is, on the stage measuring up!' remarked Sarah.

We all turned to have a good look. I could see him only from the back, but I knew straight away who he was. He was a tall, well-built man who had blond curly hair. As he turned to measure the front of the stage, I confirmed to myself that it was indeed Squire Donald McFadden, Laird of the Thistle Isles.

'Just watch and learn,' I said to my close friends, and with that, I stood on the dance floor facing Donald McFadden.

I expected a reaction from Donald, but not the one I got. As he looked up towards me and recognition set in, he jumped from the stage, ran across the dance floor, picked me up in his arms, and then the kissing started. We kissed, from seductive kissing to hard sensual kissing. I could hear my heart beating, and I could feel his heart beating. *Wow, wow, wow!* I felt those delicious sexual feelings all through my body.

'I don't believe it!' said Donald finally. 'I thought I would never see you again. What are you doing here? Please say you are a member.'

'Correct the first time,' I said, smiling at him. 'It is lovely to see you again as well.'

'Do you know why I'm here?' he asked.

'Yes, I do believe that with 54 percent of the shares, you are our new owner, with plans to match,' I said, still smiling at those bright blue eyes.

I told Donald that I would like to introduce him to some other members; namely, Sarah and Judith. My, they were surprised, and for once, they were speechless. We spent a little time catching up. Donald asked me about Thomas. I told him that we were no longer together. When he asked why, I just said, 'He did not want me!'

'The golf resort that the Hague Corporation is building in Scotland is well under way,' he said. 'The Hague family have visited Scotland a few times to check on the progress of the development. Thomas has never been with them. I think his career and interests lay elsewhere.' I nodded in agreement.

As Donald resumed his measuring, I made my exit and returned home. I was still excited about seeing Donald again. I was so looking forward to the dance and entertainment the following night. Surely, Donald would be there. That night, my thoughts kept wandering to that kissing on the dance floor. I had never experienced sexual thrills like those with any other person besides Thomas.

The following day, I was still excited about meeting Donald again. I went about my daily duties whilst planning what I was to wear, along with perfume, make-up, and jewellery options for the evening dance.

At around lunchtime, a knock came at my door. On opening my door, I was confronted with an extremely large bouquet of flowers. The delivery person said they were for a Catherine Riding. I took delivery of them, and once I had closed my door, I urgently went about trying to find a card in the midst of all the flowers. There it was. It read, 'Such a brilliant surprise to meet you again. Love, Donald x.' He must have obtained my address from the office at the golf club.

I was so thrilled to receive those flowers. I could not remember the last time anyone had ever bought me flowers.

The rest of the day, I used for resting and for getting myself good and ready for the evening. I took an extra effort in dressing and putting make-up on, doing my hair and nails, and generally making sure I looked my very best.

That evening, I arrived at the golf club by taxi. I immediately helped the bar staff and the caterers with the buffet. Most of the committee members had arrived a little early. We all met at the table nearest to the end of the bar. From there, I could monitor who arrived.

Before long, the room was full and buzzing with people. The band was quite brilliant, and a considerable number of people were actually dancing.

When Donald arrived, he was accompanied by a party of men and women. Just as I had seen before in America, they were all over Donald, especially the women. I watched him put his arms around first one and then another of these beautiful women. They were all over him, laughing and flirting with him. I likened them to clucking hens – not my sort of women, but then again, they were younger and a whole lot more attractive than I was. I felt quite deflated. Never mind – I was determined to enjoy the night.

As I stood at the bar staring at Donald, he turned, and our eyes met. Such a lovely sensation went right through me. Donald winked, and I nodded. It was some time later that Donald came over to me and asked me to dance. I thanked him for the beautiful flowers. I told him that they had really cheered me up.

As we held each other close, Donald pushed his manhood close up to me, and I could feel his excitement. I put both my arms around his shoulders, and we danced slowly, cheek to cheek. The sexual feelings were so strong between us. I was breathing his breath. As he spoke, his lips gently touched mine, setting off such a chain reaction of desire, sexual feelings, and pleasure.

'Why did you not phone me and arrange a riding lesson as you said you were going to do in America?'

'Sorry. I mislaid your card, although I have often thought of you,' I said.

'Good!' He laughed. 'I shall pick you up on Tuesday night and take you for an Indian. You do eat Indian?'

'Of course! I presume now that you have my address, and again, I thank you for those beautiful flowers.'

The evening went well. I did not see anything of Donald after that dance. I made my way home by taxi, and I looked forward to the following Tuesday night.

Tuesday evening arrived. I was well prepared and smartly, although casually, dressed. Donald arrived in a large white

Mercedes. I ran out and got into the passenger seat. He greeted me with a slow, sensual kiss, and off we went.

All night, we talked, laughed, flirted, and ate and drank. I learnt so much about this man. I remembered that I had found him rude and obnoxious in America, but he seemed the perfect gentleman with me now.

He was still single, still liked his women, and still adored his stables, horses, and foals. He was based in Scotland, where he owned a castle and a great deal of land that housed everything from public houses to farms, from village halls to housing estates. He was at Lancaster whilst he took charge of his new land purchase. He had started a small stable there, but his breeding and racing stables were in Scotland. He lived in a mansion in Scotland and a large Georgian house near Lancaster. He had beautiful bright blue eyes, lovely lips, large hands, and curly blond hair. He was strikingly handsome and very sexy.

As the night went on, I realized that he was only interested in one thing, and that was having sex with me. I made a joke telling him that I was not on the menu!

'Why not?' he asked.

'Donald, I don't know you. I am not in the habit of having sex with a stranger.'

'Of course you know me! I promise I will make you feel so good! Your place or mine?' he whispered.

The cheek of him! 'Not a chance. You have a group of clucking hens you can call upon for sex, have you not?' I whispered sarcastically.

'Ouch!' he said. 'I presume you mean my close friends. Do you not want to be one of my clucking hens, available for sex at any time?' He was very annoyed and showed it.

'I am sorry if I have annoyed you. I don't want to be disrespectful. Please forgive me!' I said quietly and apologetically.

'Apology accepted … are we going to have that riding lesson next week?'

'Most definitely. I shall look forward to it.'

He took me home, and we kissed for a long time in the car. I did not invite him in. When I left him, he said he would phone me to arrange a riding lesson for the following week.

***

It wasn't long before it was all arranged. The following Tuesday, I was to drive to his stables. I had to wear long trousers or jeans that were quite fitted, boots or heavy trainers, and a good, warm, long jumper. Donald said that he would provide the riding helmet and anything else that I might require.

We had quite a long conversation when he phoned that day. He lived in Scotland the majority of the time. He was very proud of his mansion. He was also the proud owner of an old original castle. The castle was used only as a venue for weddings, banquets, and the like, and it offered hotel accommodation for small groups.

He had recently purchased a large estate near Lancaster. Whilst he was getting his stables up and running and sorting out the farms and farm managers, he lived at The Gables. This was a six-bedroom Georgian house on the outskirts of Lancaster.

He was fascinated with the thought that I might just be able to rekindle my horse-riding skills. He thought it would be great to have me as a riding companion. I told him we would have to wait and see. We both laughed at the thought of us both riding off into the sunset.

The day arrived. Suitably dressed, I set off to drive to the stables. When I arrived, I was met by a stable girl. She told me that Donald was in the end stable, and so I walked in that direction. Donald came out to meet me.

'Come with me in here,' he said. 'I have something to show you. Be very quiet, and don't make any sudden movements,' he whispered. He took my hand and led me into a large, long stable block. At the last stable, he put both my hands onto the stable door. Standing behind me, he put his hands onto mine. As he pressed himself against my back, he whispered, 'Look into the stable. What do you see?'

The thrill of him holding me in that position had really disoriented me. I looked into the stable at the large horse, and it was a few moments before I saw the smallest of foals I had ever seen. It was lying under the mother. What a wonderful, feel-good picture! It was fantastic to see.

Donald then led me out of the stables as quietly as possible. 'The foal is a little underweight, but she has a good mother. She will be huge one day,' he said. 'Now let us see what you can do! I have a beautiful mare who follows me everywhere. She wanders around all on her own and will do only as I say. Her name is Bess. She will be perfect for you to learn on!' He had a strange glint in his eyes.

Bess was already tacked up. 'If I am not here, you will have to go into the indoor arena where there are steps to help you mount. I am here, so I will get you on your horse,' he said, laughing.

He explained that, once I had my footing in the nearest stirrup, he was going to lift me and throw me up and over the saddle. I had to stop and hold the saddle and throw my leg over into the other stirrup. I knew what he meant, as I remembered having done it so many times when I was younger.

As Donald held me, I could feel all those delicious sexual feelings again. Soon, I was sitting on Bess with no trouble at all. Donald had his mount brought out. Donald's mount was huge.

I had no trouble at all remembering how to hold the reins, how to sit, and how to control my horse and give her directions. The stable girl opened the gate, and off we went. Bess just followed Donald. We rode through the fields, side by side. In the wooded area, I followed behind him. When we reached the canal side, we dismounted. I could dismount pretty well all by myself. I was really quite pleased with myself. We never stopped talking and laughing. We really were having a good time.

After we dismounted, Donald and I just sat on a wall. With his arms around me, we kissed. He jumped off the wall and stood directly in front of me, between my legs. His hands were up my jumper, stroking and holding my breasts whilst he kissed me so seductively. I enjoyed every minute of it. As he tried to get me off the wall and down towards the grass, I had to stop him. I was not sure what he had in mind. He laughed, and he helped me mount Bess. He mounted his horse, and we made our way back along the canal side and up through the fields.

When we were back in the stable yard, the stable girl took the horses back into their stables.

'You did fantastically well today,' said Donald. 'If you can come maybe once a week for a little while, you should be able to ride all on your own in time. The stable girls will educate you in tacking up yourself. If I am not here, they will teach you all you need to know in the indoor arena. Now I will make us a late lunch. Fancy it?' he added.

'Sounds good to me. I have had such a fantastic day,' I said, holding onto Donald as we walked towards his house, The Gables.

Omelettes and salad were on the menu. Donald surprised me by making the omelettes and making the coffee himself. There was never an awkward moment between us. We seemed to feel easy in each other's company.

Donald was proud of The Gables. He showed me the large

lounge, the study, and other reception rooms. The kitchen was huge and fully kitted out.

'My housekeeper is away today. Do you want to see my bedroom upstairs?' he asked.

'Donald, stop it! You make me feel uneasy.'

'When, then?'

'I really do want to have sex with you, but I am not ready to commit myself yet. Sorry, but it does not feel right just now.' I hoped he would understand.

'I shall be back in Scotland for a while,' he said. 'Make sure you keep coming here and gaining experience. I would love to keep riding with you. It was really good today.' With that said, we walked back to my car, and I drove home.

***

Over the next few weeks, I went to the stables several times. The stable girls showed me how to tack up my horse, and they took me into the indoor arena where we practiced every movement and every control of the horse. Bess was easy; she knew what was expected of her, but I was so full of confidence that I thoroughly enjoyed my days there.

Donald phoned me quite regularly. We always had a laugh, and he made me feel so good. I really did desire him. I would think of him touching me, and all those thrills would zap through my body. I also thought of his clucking hens. They were there all the time when Donald was living here in Lancaster. Donald was such a good catch – such an eligible bachelor. I knew that Donald had his pick of any woman he wanted, and of course, he used them for his own pleasure. I just did not want to become one of those women. I wanted Donald and me to have something more. That is probably why I would not have sex with him at the moment.

*****

A few weeks later, I drove, as usual, to the stables. When I arrived, I could see that Donald's white Mercedes was parked in the car park. I was thrilled that he was back. As I entered the stable yard, Donald came to greet me. To my astonishment, he grabbed me and started kissing me in front of the staff. We seemed to be kissing each other for quite a while. Talking through our kissing, Donald said that he had really missed me and that he was always thinking of me and was so excited that he was holding me again.

'Come on, let me see what you can do all by yourself,' said Donald.

'Watch this then … I'm really going to show off now!'

'Whoa, not so fast!' said Donald, laughing, 'You won't be riding Bess.' I looked up and saw a stable girl bringing out a large horse for me to ride.

'Oh come on, that's cheating,' I shouted. 'I only know how to ride Bess!'

As Donald held me, ready to throw me up and over the

saddle, we looked in each other's eyes. There was no denying that we had something very special between us.

With Donald on his large mount, I rode the other horse brilliantly. Donald was so impressed. We headed out of the yard and down through the open fields.

'Right. Let me see what control you have. Instruct her to trot!' he shouted. I did as he instructed, and I was amazed with myself. I could trot and stop with no problem at all. I laughed, and that made Donald laugh.

'Right. Let me see you instruct her to gallop,' he shouted.

'I am not ready for that!' I shouted back.

The next thing I knew, Donald had started to gallop off down the field. My horse just had to follow, didn't it? I was holding on and trying to slow my horse down. I screamed for Donald to help me take control, but he just ignored me. I really did do very well. When I finally stopped panicking, I enjoyed the experience. As Donald pulled up in front of me, my horse decided to stop as well! I was flung forward, and how I managed to stay on that damned horse, I will never know.

Donald could not stop laughing at me. I smiled at him and said that I would get my own back one day. We had a wonderful couple of hours riding together.

When we reached the meadow area, Donald said that we could rest a while. We dismounted, and to my surprise, Donald produced a rug, which he laid on the grass.

'Where did you put that rug on your horse?' I said laughingly.

'Near the saddle, where else?' Donald replied.

As Donald lay on the rug, he said, 'Well, come on, lay down with me here. You are going to like this!'

'I will lie with you, but no funny business or else,' I said as I laughed at him as he was pulling faces at me.

As he kissed me and stroked and held my breasts under my jumper, I held him so tight with my arms around his neck. We were both enjoying each other. Donald was thrilling me all over.

'I really want to fuck you, Catherine,' Donald whispered. He continued, 'I have missed you these last few weeks.'

'I have really missed you too. I'm so pleased that I can ride your horses. I know that I have something in common with you now. I really want you to make love to me, but you don't mean here, do you?' I laughed at the thought.

'To be honest, I would fuck you anywhere, anytime,' he said, and we both laughed.

We lay on that rug with the sunshine on our faces. The birds were singing, and the atmosphere was so romantic. We lay in each other's arms, watching the white clouds drift across the blue sky.

'Come on, before I do try to fuck you,' he said, getting up and whistling for the horses to come back, as they had wandered into the meadow.

We rode for a couple of hours longer before we were back in the stable yard. 'Go and get changed, and then I will make you a late lunch,' said Donald.

I made my way to the changing rooms, but I was really struggling getting my wellington boots off. I had not borrowed that particular pair of boots before. I shouted for Donald. When he arrived, I asked him to pull the boots off. He laughed at me, and when he struggled, we were both in fits of laughter. At last, Donald managed to take both of the boots off.

It all happened so quickly. One minute, Donald was taking my boots off, then the next minute, he was kissing me and pulling my jodhpurs and knickers down. As I tried to get my balance, I fell against the large wooden bench. Donald was on top of me. His hands were up my jumper, and as he tried to get a hold of my breasts, he ripped the ribbon straps to my under slip. I tried to talk to him, but his lips were on mine all of the time. He was kissing me with a sexual urgency. I could feel the side of the wooden bench digging into my back. I knew what was going to happen. It was pointless trying to stop it from happening. Donald undid his belt and unzipped his pants. As his pants and underwear fell down, the buckle of his belt stayed at one side of me. As Donald started to have intercourse with me, the buckle began cutting into me and chaffing down one side of my stomach and round the bottom of my hip. The feeling of the intercourse sent pleasure all over my body. With him kissing me, squeezing my breasts, and moving so precisely, I knew that I was going to climax. I had a tremendous orgasm even though I was hurting from the bench and the buckle. As he kissed me, the roughness of his face chaffed the skin all down one side of my cheek and chin.

It was all over very quickly. As Donald moved off me, he saw what damage his buckle had done. I was bleeding in some places, and my skin was red raw in other places.

'Oh my God! Catherine, what have I done? I have hurt you! Mind, I will help you! Oh my God! What have I done?' exclaimed Donald, as he tried to stand me up and dress himself at the same time.

I grabbed my clothes, and Donald went outside, closing the door behind him. Through the window, I could see him just standing there, having a cigarette, and looking over the fields. I dressed myself, collected my bag, and walked outside. I was going to talk to him, but when I looked at him, there were tears running down his cheek. I just turned, went to my car, and drove home.

Once home, I ran a bath, put some antiseptic into the water, stripped off, and lay in the hot water. It had all happened so quickly that I needed time to try to remember what had actually happened. I did remember having the orgasm. *What sort of woman has an orgasm whilst being abused?* I thought to myself. I was disgusted with myself and embarrassed. I felt sorry for Donald. He had been so upset. I felt that I would never be able to face him again.

After the bath, I dressed my wounds. My back was bruised. I put a dressing on my side where the skin was badly chaffed. It was still bleeding in some places. The chaffing on my cheek and chin was becoming swollen and very red. I just broke down and cried. So now I had swollen eyes. What a mess I looked!

I could not sleep that night. I kept seeing Donald crying. I kept remembering the orgasm that I had experienced. I felt so dirty.

The next day, I phoned Sarah, Judith, and Elizabeth and told them that I had picked up a bug and that I felt severely sick and had diarrhoea. They all agreed to stay away until I was better. I did not want anyone to see me the way I was.

I never heard anything from Donald. Nothing at all. I felt used, abused, and cast aside. It took nearly two weeks for my face to look all right again.

You would think that if Donald had any decent feelings for me, he would have contacted me to see if I was alright. Well, it was obvious that he indeed had no feelings for me. He had had me sexually and had no further use of me.

As soon as I was happy with my face, I contacted my sister in Spain and asked if I could join her for a few weeks' break. My sister and her husband were delighted at the prospect of a visit. I did just that. I caught the next available flight to Girona and stayed with them for five weeks.

Those five weeks gave me time to heal, both physically and mentally. I had a lot to give to the right person, and it was my ambition to find that special person. I was not bothered about attraction or even a deep love. I just wanted to be treated with respect and love.

Before I left Spain for home, Sarah phoned and told me that an away 'hen do' had been organized for all the oldies involved in the wedding of her friend's daughter. 'Would you believe, Las Vegas?' she said. 'And the mother of one of the bridesmaids has been taken poorly, so her booking is vacant. It would cost you only seven hundred pounds to join us, if you're interested. Please do try to come. The cost is for return flights and the accommodation is at the Excalibur Hotel on the Strip. One week of fun, sun, gambling, shows, and everything else that Las Vegas can offer us! Please, please say you'll come!' Sarah sounded so excited.

'Yes, why not?' I said. 'E-mail the banking details, and I'll send the money. I could do with some fun and entertainment after spending five weeks in a quiet location in Spain!' We both laughed, and it was all settled.

The trip to Vegas was to be a week from the following weekend. I could not wait to get home and start preparing for my Vegas trip.

Chapter 8
Las Vegas

What a sight we all were. Twelve middle-aged women, all dressed in the same style of clothing – dark blue skirts and jackets with pink blouses, blue shoes, and cross over bags. We looked like a group of air hostesses. Thank goodness, we had to wear this outfit only whilst we were travelling. We were ready, and we all met at the airport.

Before long, we were landing at the airport in Las Vegas. Wow, the heat just hit us as we disembarked the plane. Transfer taxis were waiting for us. They took us to the Excalibur Hotel, and within an hour or so, we had all booked in and had taken possession of our rooms. We had six double rooms, two persons to each room. I was to share with Sarah. The rooms were gorgeous. I could not believe the size of the two beds in the room. They must have been king size! Fantastic.

Our first few days were packed full of frolic and fun. With our little buckets full of chips, we hit the casino. We ate everything we could in the buffets, and we drank everything that was offered to us. What a place. Brilliant!

Most of the shows were fully booked; in fact, some were booked up for more than a year. We managed to get tickets to the big band show at Caesar's Palace. The tickets included a five-course dinner, followed by entertainment and dancing – a chance for us all to get dressed up and show off our tans.

The evening of the show arrived. We waited patiently at the entrance to the venue. There seemed to be thousands of people there. As the doors opened, we all moved forward and tried to make our way to the area designated on our tickets. We had the necessary table number, but the venue was huge. It was like a large auditorium positioned around a large dance floor with a huge stage to one side. The sides were stepped, with tables on each level. The restrooms and bars were at the top of the tiers at the rear.

Waiters wore uniforms that were colour-coordinated according to areas of the venue. We managed to grab a waiter wearing 'our' colour, and he took it upon himself to help us find our table. He was just as lost as we were. We ended up at the edge of the dance floor, waiting for him to call us when he finally located our table. It was so ridiculous that it was funny, and we all just laughed.

The band started to play, and the master of ceremonies was waiting for everyone to be seated. I looked across the dance floor, and there he was! Judge Thomas Hague! I was quite far away from him, but I could see that he was with a woman. He was standing at the edge of the dance floor, probably as lost as we were. My heart was pounding. He turned and immediately saw me. I felt his eyes looking at me. I mimed, 'Hello, you.' Nothing. He showed no sign of recognition, but I knew that he had seen me.

Just then, a surge of people passed by, and we saw that our waiter was shouting for us. When I looked back to where Thomas had been, he was no longer there! I desperately looked around for him. Our little group finally followed our waiter, and we all settled into our seats.

All during the meal, I was up and down those steps to different restrooms, only so I could scan the tables in all of the areas. I just wanted to see him again. I wanted to talk to him. I wanted to hold him. I could not find him. By the time the meal and the entertainment had finished, I had given up trying to find him.

As I sat there, watching people dancing, someone walked up beside me and pulled on my arm.

'Would madam like to dance?' asked Thomas.

'Oh, Thomas, I have been looking for you all night!' I exclaimed with a sigh.

We walked onto the dance floor. Thomas held me so close. I put my arms around his neck, and we kissed. That kiss was so dramatic and prescious.

As we held each other, Thomas said, 'I have missed you

every day. I think of you all the time.'

'I will love you forever and a day. What are you doing here?'

'I am here to celebrate my engagement to Susan. Her family and my family are all here for a few days. Why are you here?' he asked.

'I'm with a party of twelve woman just having some fun – a week's holiday,' I replied. I could not be bothered with trying to explain what a hen do was.

'What about your husband? Are you still with him?'

'He died some time ago.'

'Why did you not contact me?' Another stupid question from Thomas.

'I tried phoning you. You no longer lived at the Miami house. I phoned your chambers and learned that you no longer preside over that court, but the person would not tell me where you had moved to. He said he'd heard that you and your wife had gone on vacation for a few weeks before you were to take up your new position. I even tried the Hague Corporation offices, but they would not give me any information about you. As I presumed that you then had a wife, I just gave up. Why, Thomas? Why did you not let me know where you were moving to?' I whispered through my teeth. I felt so angry with him.

'I assure you, Catherine, I had not got married. Yes, Susan and I moved from Florida to LA, in preparation of me taking my new position, a directorship with the Hague Corporation.'

'You say that you still think fondly of me, then why did you not have a second thought for me when you moved away?'

Thomas did not answer. He just held me close and kissed me again. The master of ceremonies was closing the show and thanking us all for being there. *Oh no,* I thought, *not yet! I need more time with Thomas.* 'Give me your phone number or at least something so that I can keep in touch with you,' I said.

'No. Sorry, Catherine. When you left, it broke me up. It is best we leave us in the past,' Thomas whispered.

'Fine!' I said, and I started to walk away from him.

'Wait, what hotel are you staying at? And what is your room number?'

'The Excalibur. Room 6067,' I replied, and we parted company.

As I made my way back to our hotel with 'the girls,' every conceivable emotion was running through my body and soul. I was so angry with Thomas. I could not understand why we could not pick up where we had left off. He did not love Susan. I knew that he still loved me, and I adored him. Why did he not want me when he could have me? What was the matter with me?

I felt so sad, so lost. I loved him. I was angry with him. I wanted him sexually. I needed him, but the truth about it all was that Judge Thomas Hague did not want me!

Back at our hotel, I had a few drinks in the bar before

retiring for the night. I needed something to help me sleep. My brain was working overtime because nothing made any sense. I wished I had never seen Thomas that night. I thought about Donald, another lover who obviously did not want me. I wished that I had never met Donald. I finally returned to my room and drifted into sleep, feeling very sorry for myself.

There is nothing worse than self-pity!

I was awakened by our hotel room phone. I knew straight away who it would be. 'Hello, you,' I answered.

Thomas laughed and said, 'It is obvious you don't know many people in Vegas.' I also laughed.

'Do you fancy going out for the day tomorrow? I thought I might take you to Lake Tahoe, and we can have a look at London Bridge. I might even buy you lunch on the lake. What do you say?'

'I would love that.'

'Be at the West Turret exit, which is at the rear of your hotel, at ten o'clock tomorrow morning. I will pick you up there, near the car park area. Wear comfortable shoes for walking, and don't forget a sun hat. Okay?'

'Yes,' I replied, still feeling angry about the way he was treating me.

'Catherine … lose the attitude!' he said as he laughed, and I laughed with him. I could not sleep that night. I was so excited about going out for the day with Thomas.

***

At ten o'clock the following morning, I waited at the West Turret exit. A limousine pulled up in front of me. The chauffeur got out and opened the rear door. Thomas was sitting in the back. I got into the car. 'What is this? I thought you were going to pick me up,' I said, a little disappointed.

'I have to travel this way. My chauffeur is also my protector, my bodyguard. He travels everywhere with me. As a person in my position with the Hague Corporation, I have to be more than careful. Don't worry; he is more than discreet.'

It was quite a journey to Lake Tahoe. We made a comfort stop halfway there – coffee and cake … *brilliant*. During the journey, as we cuddled together, Thomas told me about his situation. He told me that, after I had left him – which was so incorrect, as he had ordered me to leave – he could not function. He was so depressed. It took him weeks to get over the trauma.

Now he was to marry Susan, who had always been there for him. Susan's father had the money and connections to help get Thomas into the senate. It was his lifetime's ambition to be elected to the Senate. Being a director of the Hague Corporation, the family business, and the fact that the Corporation was doing extremely well, and that the Corporation had money to back him was all helping him achieve his lifetime's ambition to be elected to the senate.

Susan and Thomas had set their wedding day for the end of December the following year. That was over eighteen months away. He said there was no rush, and to have a large celebrity wedding, which Susan's parents wanted, it was necessary to make arrangements far in advance, as there were long waiting lists for all the best venues in Los Angeles.

'So where do you live now?' I asked.

'Susan and I have bought a house in Los Angeles.'

'I feel sick at the thought of you settling down with someone else,' I said. 'I have no chance of competing for your affections, do I?'

'Sorry, Catherine, we were in the past. I have to look to the future. I do love you. I think about you all the time, and I miss you every single day, but what can I do about it now? My choices have been taken away from me.' Thomas spoke with so much emotion that I thought he was going to break down and cry.

I held him tight, and we cuddled and kissed on the backseat of the limo. We both wanted some intimacy, but with the driver only a few feet away from us, it was out of the question. Thomas said that, even if he asked the driver to park up somewhere, he would not leave us alone. So we just did what we could without going too far sexually.

When we arrived at the lake, we could see the riverboats. 'I shall take you on one of those boats, and I shall buy you lunch on it,' exclaimed Thomas.

'Yes, I would really enjoy that,' I replied, all excited.

For over two hours, we were on the riverboat. We passed

London Bridge and sailed up and down the lake. Lunch was fantastic. We sat opposite each other. Just looking into each other's eyes was sending thrills all over each of us. We acted like lovers. We felt like lovers. We talked, we laughed, we kissed, and we flirted.

Before long, we were in the car getting ready to return to Vegas. We curled up together on that backseat.

'What is going to happen to us?' I asked him.

'There is nothing that can happen with us. As I said, we were in the past, Catherine. What can I do now? I am so sorry, but that is how it is.' He spoke quietly.

'It seems so wrong!' I whispered to him, but I still held him tight. I did not want to ever let him go. With that said, we both fell asleep in each other's arms.

I woke up as Thomas was telling me that we had arrived back at my hotel. The chauffeur opened the door for me. I just got out of the car and walked straight into the hotel through the exit doors. I could not say goodbye. I just wanted to forget that I ever knew him.

I joined the girls for a really good night out. I was just going to forget Thomas Hague.

***

It was in the early hours of the morning that our hotel room phone rang. Sarah was fast asleep, and again, I knew who it was, and so I answered, 'Hello, you.' Thomas laughed and said, 'Listen carefully. Leave your room, turn right, walk until you find the lift on the left-hand side. Get in the lift, go up one floor, exit, and turn right. Walk down the corridor to room 7060. I am waiting for you.'

'I am on my way,' I screeched – quietly – with delight.

I followed the directions and entered room 7060 through the door, which was ajar, straight into Thomas's arms.

'Do you remember me saying a long time ago that I wanted to share your bed for a couple of hours or so as I intended to fuck you?' asked Thomas.

'Yes. I will never forget. That was the first day I met you.'

'Well, tonight, my lady, I intend to fuck you,' whispered Thomas.

That night was a night of passion. We both desired each other. We had sex with passion and pleasure, but most of all, we loved each other. Every touch, lick, bite, kiss, and stroke meant so much more to us than just having sex. We knew how much we loved each other.

But, finally, it was time for Thomas to leave and return to Susan.

'Please give me some contact information,' I begged. 'I will be heartbroken to think that I will never be able to contact you again.'

'That is not possible. I thought I had explained my situation. It is best that we just go our separate ways. Sorry, Catherine, we cannot bring back what we have lost. I will always love you, and I will always have you in my heart.'

I put my face in the pillow. I did not want to see him leave. I heard the door close, and he was gone!

I stayed in that room until mid-morning, giving the girls the chance to leave our rooms and go for breakfast. I did not want to see anybody.

At my age, I should be enjoying life. All I seemed to experience was heartache. All caused by men. Selfish men. Well, that was going to change. To hell with Thomas Hague! He has just used me. *To hell with Donald McFadden! He also used me. It is about time that I took control of my future. To make myself happy, I want to marry a man who loves me and is reasonably wealthy. That is my goal – to find such a man. To hell with being in love with him!*

What had happened to the fun-loving, hardworking lover of life that I used to be? I knew what had happened – Thomas Hague had happened. He was still breaking my heart. *Enough! Enough!* I had to start changing my attitude about how I was to live my life.

I needed a husband who loved me and whom I loved back. I needed someone to take care of me and someone I could take care of. I needed passion in my life. I was so down and heart-broken that I said a small prayer to my dead husband, Richard. I knew that all my mixed up feelings were probably due to the fact that I might not have gotten over his death. I said, 'I am on a roller coaster that is taking me down and down. I don't know how to stop it or jump off it. I feel lost with no purpose to hang on to. I feel that I have lost everything that matters. Help me, please!'

Our hotel room was empty; Sarah must have gone to breakfast. I had a shower, got changed, and with make-up all done, nails done, dressed to kill, I went to find the girls. From now on, it was going to be smiles all the time, no matter how I felt.

What a brilliant afternoon and night we all had. I really enjoyed myself. We made our way back to our rooms, exhausted. Some of us had won money; others had lost money. But none of us cared. We had enjoyed the experience. We all had to pack, as we were to leave the following morning for the airport and the flight home.

With packing all done, I curled up in my large king-sized bed. I was awakened again by the hotel room phone. No way, I thought to myself. *Thomas has said his goodbyes.* I answered the phone with an abrupt 'Yes?'

'That sounds as if there is a problem,' said Thomas.

'Yes, there is a problem,' I said quickly.

'Come to the same room as last night. I need to see you before we both leave. If there is a problem, I will sort it. Come on, Catherine. I am waiting for you,' said Thomas.

'No, I don't think so,' I replied.

'Why?' asked Thomas.

'I don't want to! You said your goodbyes last night. Your

words are worthless. You have used me. I wish I had never met you!' I hissed the words out.

There was a silence between us, and I said, 'Thomas …'

'Yes?'

'Goodbye, Thomas. Fuck off!' With that said, I put the phone down and returned to my bed to try and get some sleep before we started our long journey home.

Chapter 9
A New Start

Home at last! I was so happy to be back in my own home. It did not take me long to unpack. It was about seven o'clock in the evening, but I was so tired that I curled up in my own comfortable bed and went to sleep. I slept solidly, and I was surprised to find that it was dawn nearly two days later when I woke up.

The days that followed were full of friends and family. At last, I was beginning to appreciate what I had. I had money in the bank, my own house, wonderful friends, beautiful daughters, a good son, and an appetite for life.

'The golf club is having a talent night on Friday,' said Sarah. 'Will you be available to help? It should be a really good night.'

'Yes, of course. I will look forward to it.' I might have been looking forward to it, but I was dreading meeting Donald. How was I to face him? I was just hoping that he would not be there that night.

I had made myself a promise – nothing was ever going to bother me again. I was going to go after what I wanted, and to hell with any consequences. I found that I had some inner strength, so why should I be bothered about Squire McFadden?

***

As I arrived at the golf club on the evening of the talent night, I was surprised at how beautiful the old building looked. It sat in the centre of a mass of landscaped gardens. As the sun set over the golf course and the clubhouse, I sat on one of the benches and collected all my thoughts. For the first time in a long time, I was looking forward to my future, whatever it might have in store for me.

It was good to be back in the club. Paul, the head barman, was pleased to see me and bought me a drink. I stood talking to him for quite a while. The biggest news story he had for me was that Sheila Jones had moved in with Squire McFadden at The Gables. That news did not bother me at all.

Just then, there was Donald McFadden, on the stage, with the microphone. So he was the master of ceremonies for the night. There were six acts taking part in the talent competition. All of them were music acts – two solo artists, two bands, and two duets. There were to be three judges, and all of them were sitting by the stage. The dance floor was open to all who fancied dancing. Sarah had arranged the interval buffet, so all in all, it was going to be an interesting night.

It was not long before Donald saw me. A quick nod of acknowledgement was all he gave me. He was a striking figure of a man – tall and handsome with blond curly hair. I knew that he had the most beautiful blue eyes. I also knew that he had beautiful large hands. The thought of those hands sent shivers down my spine. I knew that I still found him sexually attractive. Watching him gave me those delicious sexual feelings. *Be sensible*, I thought to myself.

As the evening progressed, Donald was fantastic as the master of ceremonies. He told jokes and good-naturedly made fun of some of the people in the room and some of the artists. I laughed so much it made me feel good.

Halfway through the talent competition, one of the judges declared that she was unwell and asked to be excused. As she left her judge's seat, over the microphone, Donald asked if his 'Lady Catherine' would be kind enough take over the vacant position. Obviously, with all eyes watching me, I had no choice but to oblige, and so I took my place in the judge's seat. The competition continued.

It was easy to see how the judges were marking each act. I continued to mark as they all did.

After all the acts had taken part, disco music took over. Donald came over to us and asked for our results. As he leaned across me, I blew my breath across his neck. He looked shocked and surprised. I just smiled at him. All of a sudden, he was kissing me. Only a short kiss, but all the old feelings were there. He looked confused, and I just smiled at him.

Our work was done. We had chosen the first-place winner, the runner up, and the third-place winner. Donald then did his final act of the night, and that was to announce these results. I returned to the bar and ordered myself a large brandy and soda. I needed it!

The evening, for me, was a great success. I danced with a couple of men. I ate lovely food from the buffet and had a few more drinks. I never once looked over to where Donald stood with Sheila and a few more of his clucking hens.

Before I left for home in a taxi, I went outside to smoke my artificial cigarette. Donald was there, smoking and talking with some men friends. I thought to myself, *Well, go for it!*

I walked over to him and asked him if he had a minute. I was not nervous at all; in fact, I felt that I was in full control of the situation. He followed me to a quieter place, and with no warning, I placed my hands round his neck and kissed him ever so seductively. Of course, he responded with an urgency that resulted in us kissing and holding each other tight for quite a while. He thrilled me all over. I felt that I needed more and more of Squire Donald McFadden. When we pulled apart, I whispered, 'Come home with me and spend the night.'

'Don't play me, Catherine!' he whispered back.

'I am so serious,' I said, smiling and looking deep into his beautiful eyes.

'Sorry, I can't tonight. I have made arrangements.' He looked very apologetic.

'Which clucking hen have you chosen to play with to-night?' I hissed at him. I turned and walked away. I was not bothered at all. I would give him one last chance. I walked back to him and whispered, 'I will leave my door open all night if need be. If you want me, you know where I am.' With that, I walked away and joined Paul at the bar.

***

The taxi took me home. I made myself some coffee and made the bedroom look inviting. I smiled to myself. I knew he would come. With a silk slip on, the bed turned down, music on the radio, and a good book in my hands, I curled up on the bed.

It was not long before I heard the front door open and close. Donald ran upstairs and stood there looking at me. 'Right, lady,' he said. 'Just tell me what your game is. I am still mortified by our episode months ago. It made me feel ill. I still have not got over the trauma it had caused me. I would never hurt you on purpose. You made a fool of me … never again.'

'I made a fool of you?' I shouted. 'I hid away for a long time with a badly bruised and swollen face. Is that making a fool of you?'

'You climaxed, didn't you? I felt it in you! You were to blame as much as I was!' Donald retaliated. 'I think it would be best that I tell you that Sheila has moved in with me at The Gables.'

I remained silent. I was in no way upset. He could think and believe what he wanted. To hell with him. If he wanted to stay in my bed, that would be brilliant. But if he didn't, he could rot in hell for all I cared!

'Well, my Lady Catherine, have you nothing to say?' Donald said quietly.

'No. Are you going to make love to me or not?' I said quietly.

That night was a night to remember. We made love over and over again. We held each other as lovers do. We enjoyed each other. Eventually, we fell asleep in each other's arms. As morning came, Donald left my house. I did not speak to him, and he did not speak to me. There were no goodbyes. I knew that Donald McFadden was mine. It was a bittersweet feeling.

At nine o'clock that morning, my phone rang. It was Donald calling. I ignored it. At eleven o'clock, my phone rang again. It was Donald calling. I ignored it. At twelve o'clock, my phone rang. It was Donald calling. This time I answered it. 'Hello, you,' I said.

'Well, why have you been ignoring my calls? You had better have a bloody good explanation!'

'I was giving you time,' I replied softly.

'Time for what?' said an irate Donald.

'If you don't know, I am not going to tell you. It does not matter anyway.' I spoke very softly. That would give him something to think about. I smiled at the thought of Donald trying to work me out.

'Pack a suitcase. I will pick you up later today. Probably around five.'

'Where are we going?'

'Back to my home in Scotland, of course. Heatherfield Country Manor. See you later, and be ready!' And with that, he rang off.

I had been trying to confuse him, but now I was totally confused myself. Was I to go with him? Too bloody right I was!

***

With my suitcase packed and ready in the hall, I turned off all services, like water and electricity. As I stood in the kitchen, Donald came running in. I laughed as he came towards me. He was looking so excited. 'From this day forth, you shall be known as my Lady Catherine. I shall love and protect you until the day I die. That is quoted on the large tapestry in the old castle hall,' he said.

'I thought you were saying that to me!' I said.

'I just have!' retorted Donald. 'Now, are you ready for a great adventure?' he said. We kissed and held each other tight. 'Come on. No time to waste.'

As we travelled towards Scotland, I watched all the fields, trees, water, and villages pass us by.

'That was some sex session last night, was it not?' asked Donald.

'Are you complaining?'

'No way!'

'You were fantastic … bloody fantastic,' I said.

'I know. I know,' he replied, and we both laughed.

It was going to be quite a few hours' journey, so I asked Donald to tell me all about his estate and the life he led there.

He told me that his property covered a huge area – three villages, six farms, the estate farm, stables, a castle that was used as a hospitality venue and hotel, a loch, and a river full of trout. He lived in a large Georgian mansion called Heatherfield Country Manor. It had numerous en suite bedrooms, and it was home to two beautiful four-legged friends. He employed numerous staff, a housekeeper called Mrs. Bumble – Babs for short, although he suggested that I treat her with respect and call her Mrs. Bumble – two house maids, three groundsmen, four stable staff, and a game keeper. He also employed a farm manager, a stable manager, and a secretary who knew everything. According to Donald, he could not function without her. Apparently, she did everything that he should do. The whole of his estate was run by the estate manager, who in turn had his own secretary.

Donald had sold one of the Thistle Islands and a considerable amount of land on the mainland to the Hague Corporation. They were to build a golf resort and spa. That is why he had been in America when I met him at the Hagues' golden wedding celebrations.

'The Hague Corporation has built a bridge from the mainland and have nearly completed the clubhouse and hotel. I will take you there and show you what a masterpiece it really is,' Donald said.

'Do the Hagues ever come over here?' I asked.

'Yes, quite often.'

I had to ask – 'Does Thomas Hague ever come over?'

'No. He has other interests elsewhere. I want to know – now be honest with me – why do you want to know about Thomas Hague? You don't still think about him, do you?'

'No. I am just curious.'

Donald pointed out the window. 'There, in the distance, you can see the castle, and to the right of it, you can see the manor,' he said.

We entered the grounds through a massive wrought iron gate. I was feeling so nervous, but I was also very excited. As we pulled up in front of the mansion, a groundsman came to meet us, and Donald instructed him to take my suitcase indoors. As the front door was opened, out came bounding – and I mean bounding – two golden retrievers. All they wanted was affection from Donald, and all Donald wanted was affection from them. I tried to stroke them, but they did not want anything to do with me.

We entered through the front entrance, straight into a huge hallway. It was big enough to be used as a dance floor! All the wooden panelling had been painted white. Polished wooden floors led from the hallway into each adjoining room. A large staircase wound round and upwards to the first floor area. A large chandelier hung majestically in the centre of the hall.

'Follow me. We'll find Babs, and hopefully, our evening meal,' Donald said, laughing.

We entered the large kitchen. The dining table, at one end of the kitchen, looked as if it could seat at least ten persons. The kitchen seemed to house every conceivable appliance that there could be.

'Babs!' shouted Donald.

In through another entrance came Babs. She was a stocky older woman who looked quite stern.

'This is my Lady Catherine,' said Donald. 'Whatever she wishes, you will supply.' He looked at me. 'Catherine, this is Mrs. Bumble, Babs for short,' he said. 'Are we to eat soon?' he asked Babs. She smiled and turned her attention back to preparing the food.

We sat at the huge table. Donald made me a coffee and remarked about how quiet I seemed.

'It is far too much for me to take in,' I said. 'I feel very tired.'

'Things will look different in the morning. You are too tired because of last night,' Donald remarked.

I could feel myself blush. 'You are supposed to be making me feel comfortable,' I said, scolding him. Donald laughed at my uneasiness.

The two dogs were called Jeremy and Jess. They never left Donald's side. When Donald sat at the table, they both lay at his feet. When Donald got up to get something, they followed by his side.

Babs had prepared a great evening meal for us. I had lost my appetite, but I made sure I ate something as a sign of thanks and respect.

'Do I put your Lady Catherine in the pink suite?' asked Babs.

'No … I told you that Catherine will be in my room and in my bed. Don't ever embarrass Catherine again. Do you hear me?' said an angry Donald.

'Sorry, sir. I just thought that she would be more comfortable in her own room. I will make sure her suitcase is taken to your room.'

Then I did feel uncomfortable. I was relieved when Donald said he would take me upstairs to our room. I just wanted to get away from that kitchen area. Donald disappeared as soon as he had taken me into his room.

Donald's room was a typical man's room. It was very dark outside, so all the curtains were closed. Forget unpacking. I was so tired, and I felt a little upset. I went into the bathroom, had a quick wash, and cleaned my teeth the best way I could, and then undressed, found a shirt in Donald's wardrobe to wear, and finally collapsed into the large, king-sized bed.

I must have fallen asleep. Donald woke me as he climbed into bed with me. He cuddled me and said, 'You will feel so much better tomorrow. It has been a long day, and I could tell you felt uncomfortable when we arrived here. I promise that you will really enjoy your stay here.'

We fell asleep in each other's arms. In the middle of the night, I crept out of bed and into the bathroom. I was desperate to go to the loo. The dogs were lying on the floor, and they made me jump. When I returned, I found I had awakened Donald. He helped me back into bed but asked me to take the shirt off and lie on my stomach with my hands held out to my sides. At first, I laughed and refused, but he said that he was not going to hurt me and for me to do as I was told. I was too tired to object and so did as he requested.

It was really weird. Donald stroked and felt all of my body. When he had finished with my back, he turned me over and instructed me to lie as before with my hands out to the side. Again, he stroked and felt every area of my body. Everywhere! If I made any small movement, he stopped as if to memorise that area. It was as if he was mapping my whole body. I found this very sensual. When he had finished, he put the shirt back on me, cuddled up to me, and we both went back to sleep.

The next morning, I woke up to the sun shining through the curtains. The birds were singing, and the dogs were trying to climb onto the bed. I tried to stroke the dogs, but all they wanted was Donald, who was still asleep with his head under the pillows. The dogs were having none of it and desperately tried to dig Donald's head out from underneath the pillows. Within minutes, Donald was rolling about with them.

'Come on! Join in if you dare to!' Donald was laughing.

'I don't think they want me here, so I will miss out on playing with them if you don't mind,' I said.

Donald let the dogs out of the room and cuddled and kissed me. He knew how to thrill me, and I hoped I knew how to thrill him. No problem there then.

'I will shower first and get out of your way. When you are ready and unpacked, make your way downstairs. I will be down in the kitchen. A good breakfast will do us both good. Just move my clothes out of the way to make room for yours. You know, Catherine, I have never had a woman stay in my room before. So, it is just as strange for me as it is for you, but we are going to have such fun, aren't we? The answer to that is yes!' We both laughed.

When Donald had left the room, I opened the curtains. Wow – four large windows looked over some of the most spectacular views I had ever seen. I could see all the landscaped gardens. I could see the hills in the distance. The sun was shining, and I felt good.

I unpacked as instructed. Showered and dressed, with make-up on, hair done, and sensible shoes on my feet, I was looking forward to exploring the grounds.

I found my way down stairs and into the kitchen. The dogs came to greet me. How they didn't manage to knock me over, I will never know.

'Good morning, Lady Catherine,' said Mrs. Bumble, with a smile on her face.

Had I walked into a different, but parallel, universe?

I smiled and returned her greeting. Donald was too interested in his morning newspapers to notice anything.

'Help yourself to what is set out for breakfast. If you want anything different, let me know,' said Mrs. Bumble.

'I have told the stables to be ready for us after lunch. Is that all right with you, my beautiful Lady Catherine?' joked Donald. I just nodded.

After breakfast, Donald and I and the dogs walked through the gardens. I held onto his arm, and we acted as any lovers would.

After a light lunch in the kitchen, Donald took me to the stables. There was a walkway that led from the house to the stables. The stables were huge. In every field surrounding the stables, there were horses. Donald introduced me to all the stable staff and instructed them to fetch the horses that had been prepared for us. They were magnificent.

'Madam,' said one of the stable girls, 'we have put aside

some riding clothes and gear for you. They should fit all right, but if they don't, let me know. We should have something else we can try.'

Donald interrupted her and said he would prefer that they called me Lady Catherine and not madam.

After I changed into the riding clothes, which fit perfectly, Donald did his usual 'up and over' routine to help me onto my horse. Once I was seated, he mounted his large horse, and off we went through the rear gate of the stables. The dogs never left Donald's side.

We spent all afternoon exploring his estate. When we reached the river, we stopped, dismounted, and walked slowly, with the dogs by our side, talking and laughing together. I was so proud of myself for being able to prove that I was a competent rider, and I had not made a fool of myself in front of the stable staff. Donald was well impressed. It was a thoroughly enjoyable experience.

When we returned to the manor, I showered and changed for the evening.

The day ended with another brilliant evening meal from Mrs. Bumble. We retired to a large lounge where a roaring fire awaited us. Donald sat at a table to do some paperwork, and I curled up on one of the large sofas to watch television. Jeremy and Jess, the dogs, stayed by Donald's side. A couple of large brandies made the evening magical.

Retiring to bed with Donald felt so normal. We were so

at ease with each other's company. We could spend hours not speaking to each other, and we could spend time talking, laughing, and flirting with each other. To make love to Donald was so easy. There was no stress, just pure enjoyment. I enjoyed him, and he enjoyed me, but the best thing of all was being able to curl up with him and for us to go to sleep in each other's arms.

***

Several days after we had arrived at the manor, I found a large parcel on our bed, tied up in blue ribbon.

'Open it!' said Donald.

I opened the parcel, and inside it, I found a complete riding outfit, including helmet, gloves, boots, and socks.

'That is a lovely present. How did you know what sizes to buy?' I asked.

'I know everything about you. I know every inch of you.' He laughed.

We took trips out in his Mercedes, from village pubs to seaside ice cream parlours, from shopping malls to tours of fish farms. We covered and saw everything there was to be seen and done.

The visit to the proposed Thistle Golf, Hotel, and Spa Resort was quite spectacular. This was the development of the Hague Corporation. It was nearing completion, but the finishing touches were a long way from being done. I was taken aback when I saw the marble entrance hall. On one wall hung photographs of all the members of the Hague Corporation. I stood there, staring at Thomas Hague. I felt physically sick. I really loved that man! That man, Thomas Hague, loved me but did not want me! I would always be in his debt, and I would never forget how he helped me when I most needed help. Why could he not have loved me enough to take a chance on us? Well, I would never know the answer to that, so I just put all my feelings and memories away to one side, away from my heart and my soul. I would not let myself think about him, even though it had been quite a shock to see his photograph there on display.

The most memorable place Donald took me to was the castle that sat proudly on a hill on his land. It had been restored and made into a hotel and a venue for weddings and other events. What a beautiful place it was, and so much history. Donald was correct when he said there was a tapestry in the large hall that had these words woven into it: 'From this day forth, you shall be known as my Lady Catherine. I will love you and protect you until the day I die.'

Donald gave me a full tour of the castle. From the outside, it looked huge. A dry moat surrounded it. I suppose that at one time, the moat would have been full of water. A bridge made an entrance, and a stone road led visitors into the central courtyard. The restoration had allowed for two large venue rooms, each with a stage and a large dance floor. It accommodated a restaurant, which was used mainly as a breakfast room for overnight guests. On the first floor, there were a total of ten-bedroom suites, each to accommodate two persons. To the rear of the castle was the most interesting area where the rooms were old and untouched. The rooms were small and filled with old wooden furniture – all originals. There was a large dining hall with a table that must have seated at least twenty people in the olden days. A smaller hall was outfitted with seats and pews, and it was in this room that the tapestry was housed. I read those beautiful words again. 'Who was Lady Catherine?' I asked.

'Not a clue,' answered Donald. 'It has been here forever. We have had to have it preserved. I'm not sure, but I think she was beheaded because she did not do as she was told or something like that. So beware!' He laughed.

'When I get some time, I am going to do some research on that tapestry,' I announced.

All around the castle were large spotlights, which were lit every night. They gave such a fantastic eerie and romantic feel to the castle and the grounds.

By the time day four of my visit had arrived, I knew Heatherfield Country Manor pretty well. When Donald had to go to work, I was able to walk the gardens, visit the stables, and even take the dogs for a walk to the river and beyond. The dogs became my best friends and never left my side once Donald was out of sight. In the evening, in the lounge, the dogs had started to be my best friends. In fact, all they wanted to do was lie with me in front of the open fire. I knew my way about the house, and Mrs. Bumble had insisted that I call her Babs. Babs became quite a friend to me. She loved to hear about my culinary disasters, and she would laugh and make fun of me. We became quite close although Donald was not so pleased about it.

Donald and I had days full of enjoyment. From the minute we woke in the morning to the minute we fell asleep at night, we had such a close relationship. I loved Donald, but I was in love with Thomas Hague. I knew that I would love Thomas Hague forever and a day.

Soon, it was time for Donald to take me back home. We timed our trip back around his required visit to his small estate near Lancaster. I never asked him about Sheila, as it was none of my business, and Donald never discussed her with me.

***

Soon, I was back home. By the time I had unpacked and lit the fire, made a brew, and phoned close family members and friends, I felt as if I had never been away. Donald said that he would keep in touch with me. His visits to the Lancaster estate were to become less frequent as he had secured a farm manager and a stable manager, and there was no need for him to be there so often. For the time being, he was to keep The Gables for himself. It made a good base for him, and he was comfortable there.

After he had taken me home, he was to stay at The Gables. I knew that he was looking forward to meeting up with his man mates and his clucking hens, and I presumed, Sheila as well. I felt a little uncomfortable about it all, but Donald and I had never pretended to have anything more than just a very close, intimate relationship.

It took Donald nearly a week before he phoned me to see how I was and just have a brief conversation. I was not bothered, but I did feel a little left out of his life. I thought that he might have treated me with a little love, attention, and respect. *How wrong I was!* I knew that I had to rise above any smouldering jealous feelings that I might have. If I wanted him, then it was up to me to make a move on him. If he turned me away, then I would know once and for all that I was just being used. The only problem was that I did not want him, so why was I bothered about what should be or shouldn't be? Let him have his clucking hens – and I presumed women in Scotland too – to play with.

My sister and her husband wanted to know if I wanted to spend some time with them in Spain before they came home for the winter. Yes, I thought to myself. *It would get me away for a few weeks and give me a good tan before I came back for the winter months.* I packed straight away and flew out to Girona. I was going to be out there only for four weeks as Margaret and Matt were going to come back home for the winter months.

Donald phoned me a few times while I was in Spain. He was his usual spoilt, obnoxious self, but he never failed to make me laugh. At least, we were good friends, and Donald told me that he was looking forward to meeting up with me again when I returned home. That never happened for months to come.

I returned home in time for the winter months. Christmas and the New Year were just around the corner. Donald was back in Scotland for the winter, and of course, for Christmas and Hogmanay – the Scots word for the last day of the year. I enjoyed all the festive parties at the golf club, and of course, at Sarah's and Judith's homes. I also went to stay with my daughter, Carol, and her partner in their new home. My other daughter, Jennifer, joined us, and it was brilliant for us all to be together. I was not sure where Tony was. He had been travelling, and we had last heard from him when he was in Costa Rica. I had received postcards from him, so I knew he was all right.

On Christmas Eve, I received a large bouquet of flowers from Donald. The card read, 'From the person who loves you the most.' The cheek of it! But it made me smile. That was followed up with a phone call at ten minutes past midnight on New Year's Eve. It was the Hogmanay celebration in Scotland, and I knew that Donald would be dressed up in his kilt and all his finery and would be partying with all his friends and family, so to receive a call from him at just passed midnight was a shock to me.

'Happy New Year, my beautiful Lady Catherine!' Donald said. 'I really wish you were here with me now!'

'Happy New Year to you too,' I replied. 'And I am glad that I am not with you now as you all sound as if you are drunk!'

'Where are you?' asked Donald.

'I am at the New Year's Eve dinner-dance at your golf club. You should be here with me, not there in Scotland,' I said, laughing.

When people around realized I was talking to Donald, they all started shouting Happy New Year to him. 'Can you hear them all?' I asked Donald.

He laughed and said, 'Yes. Same to them. I miss you, Catherine. I wish I was sleeping with you tonight. Not that we would get much sleep. Have to go! Love you!' Then, he rang off. I did not hear from him much after that.

***

It was coming up to Easter, and the golf club staff had arranged the yearly coach trip to the races. I was determined not to miss this event. I knew that I would see Donald there as he had horses entered in the races. There must have been around forty of us from the golf club. I believe that Donald knew that we would all be there, and he had arranged passes for us all in the owner's enclosure. Great or what? I knew that I would definitely be seeing him, and I was very excited about that!

The day of the races arrived. I could not have looked any better than I did. I had really gone to town with a new, short haircut, new clothes, new perfume, and hopefully, a new attitude.

We were all admitted to the owners' enclosure, and after walking around with a few of our party, we all placed bets on the upcoming races. I knew nothing about horse racing and betting, but it was fun learning what to do. I laughed at Sarah's attempt at placing a bet.

Before long, I caught sight of Donald, surrounded by his

man mates and, of course, his clucking hens. I also noticed that he was holding onto Sheila. I felt so deflated and disappointed. *Well, he is not going to ruin my day,* I thought to myself. I carried on enjoying the experience and meeting new people. I completely ignored Donald, his man mates and clucking hens, and, of course, Sheila.

Before long, I could see Donald making his way over to our party. I stood back against the fence and away from the rest of the group. He walked passed everyone and straight over to me. He just stood there, looking into my eyes. *Oh, those beautiful blue eyes!* I could feel my heart beating faster and faster. I could feel those delicious sexual feelings running through my body.

'What?' I asked.

'Nothing. Just wanted to see if you still fancied fucking me,' said Donald.

'Why are you so rude and uncouth?' I said angrily.

He placed his hands around my back, pulled me towards him, and kissed me. I kissed him back – a long, hard, sensual kiss. *Wow, I had forgotten how good he felt.* I could taste and smell him, and I could feel his manhood pressed up against me. Every part of me ached for him sexually.

'Don't move yet until I have composed myself,' whispered Donald.

'You have an audience, Donald – mainly your clucking hens and, of course, Sheila,' I whispering through my teeth.

'When you get home, pack your suitcase. I am taking you back to Scotland with me tomorrow.' He held me tight.

'Don't you think that you should ask me first?'

'No. I am telling you, and that is enough,' he said as he let go of me.

Donald turned around and went over to talk to the rest of our party. I just stood there, not knowing if he was serious or not about taking me to Scotland. I watched him leave with his stupid party of man mates and clucking hens and, of course, Sheila. I made my way to the toilets to freshen up and then made my way to the bar area. This was the time to have a few drinks! Who does he think he is ordering me about?

As I stood by the bar, Donald came over to me. 'Have I upset you, my beautiful Lady Catherine?' he said.

'Get lost, Donald. I am not interested in your games. I am disappointed in you. I thought you could, at least, treat me with some respect.' I spoke quietly and added, 'I do not want to come to Scotland with you. I do not want to be used for your entertainment. I am not one of your clucking hens, and I never will be.' I was defiant.

'My best friend, William, is to wed next weekend. I am to be his best man. The service is to be at the church on the estate, and the reception is to be held at the castle. I need you by my side. You are the only woman I will feel comfortable with on this very special occasion. Please say that you will be my plus one. I really want you to come. I have missed you, and I have missed sex with you.' Donald looked straight into my eyes, and then he started pulling faces at me.

He made me smile. 'I will think about it,' I replied.

'Good, pick you up at ten. Be ready. Pack an evening dress as well as a wedding outfit,' he said, laughing as he walked away.

I did not see him again that day. Our entire coach party had a fantastic day. When we returned to the bar at the golf club, we all had tales to tell of the winners that did not win. We all laughed at some of the tales that were told.

Finally, I was back home. I was tired and a little excited at the prospect of maybe going back to Heatherfield Manor. Was I to go or not? Of course, I was to go. I half packed a suitcase and then fell into bed exhausted.

By the time Donald arrived the next morning, I was fully prepared – all packed and the house all ready to be locked up and made secure. He came running in, all excited as he had done once before. We hugged and kissed. Again, we set off on that beautiful journey to Scotland!

I sat in the passenger seat of Donald's white Mercedes, watching him drive. He was such a striking figure of a man – handsome and sexy. I would have loved to have thought that, perhaps, he loved me, but with all the women he knew and played with, I knew I could not really be in the running for his total love and affection.

As before, I watched all the fields, villages, trees, hills, and water pass by. This time, I was not nervous at all. I was so looking forward to being at the manor, and of course, I was so looking forward to sharing Donald's bedroom and bed.

Having set off on our journey in the morning, we would arrive mid-afternoon, where before we had set off in the evening and had only arrived later at night.

'You seem very quiet, my beautiful Lady Catherine. Is there something wrong that I don't know about?' asked Donald.

'No, but while you ask, I am concerned about Bess. You don't go and see her as much now. Can you not arrange for her to be brought back here to you?' I asked.

'What will you do for me if I do that for you?' asked Donald, smirking.

'What do you want?' I replied.

'I want your undivided love and affection for the full three weeks,' he replied.

'Three weeks!' I shouted. 'You must be joking. You never said anything about three weeks!'

'The wedding is next Saturday. It will be a great day. I have been friends with William since we were little nippers at infant school. We have done everything together, and we are inseparable. I was thrilled when he asked me to be his best man. Ann, his bride to be, was not so pleased, but it had nothing to do with her.'

'Sounds as if this Ann does not like you. Why?' I asked.

'Perhaps it is because I keep taking William to gentleman-only clubs, or perhaps it is because I keep introducing him into the circle of women I play with, or perhaps it is because I am always getting him drunk or … do you get the idea?'

'You are a bad influence. That is why she does not like you.'

'Correct.' He laughed. 'Now, I know that I am not a considerate man. I don't mean to be awkward. It is just that I am so busy I don't think, and I don't make allowances for things.'

'Such as?'

'Such as … I have to leave you on your own tonight. I have arranged for a stag night for William with all our mates. Sorry! I will make it up to you! Is that okay?'

'I am not bothered. I am going to look through some of your old history books in the library and see if I can find any reference to a Lady Catherine. I have tried the Internet, and I have found nothing.'

'When you are in the library, can you write me a best man's speech?' asked Donald, pulling his face at me.

'Get lost! Do your own dirty work, as it will be dirty, won't it?'

'Oh! You know me so well, my beautiful Lady Catherine.' We both laughed.

'Where are you going to take everyone tonight?' I asked.

'Well, it goes along the lines of … getting all dressed up, a few local drinks, a meal, a nightclub, the casino, a gentlemen-only club, getting drunk, having a fight, and getting arrested for disturbing the peace, or something similar.' Donald laughed.

'No wonder Ann doesn't like you!'

The journey seemed to take longer this time. We took a couple of comfort stops, as I needed the loo, and we both had a coffee. We arrived mid-afternoon. At last, we were turning into the long drive up to the manor. One of the groundsmen was driving towards us in a pick-up. He waved to me, and I smiled and waved back. Donald stared at me, and I said, 'What?'

As we pulled up at the large front door, another groundsman came to help us with my luggage. 'I will take your luggage, Lady Catherine,' he said. Donald stared at me again, and again I said, 'What?'

Over in the gardens, a young apprentice gardener waved, so I waved back. Donald stared at me again, and again I said, 'What?'

As Donald opened the large front door, the two dogs, Jeremy and Jess, came bouncing out. They passed and ignored Donald and came straight to me to greet and love me. Donald stared at me, and I laughed and said, 'What?'

I walked through the large entrance hall and straight into the kitchen. Babs and I greeted one another warmly. 'It is lovely to see you again,' she said. 'I will make you a good, welcoming meal tonight.'

'Brilliant,' I said. 'Don't bother making Donald anything. He is going out tonight and will be eating out, that is if he has time!' Again, Donald stared at me. 'What?' I said, and we both started to laugh.

I ran up the large staircase to our room. I wanted to freshen up and change before the evening meal. After a shower, I started to unpack. Donald came into the room with only one thing on his mind.

'Right, Lady. You seem to be very at home here. How's about you come and give me a greeting I won't forget!' demanded Donald.

'Talk about a gentleman-only club. Watch this space!' I said as I slowly took off all my clothes. 'Take your clothes off and sit on this chair,' I instructed Donald. This, he did with relish. I then stood astride the chair and slowly lowered myself onto Donald's erect penis. Facing him, I kissed him. I felt his lips with my tongue, and I made sure that he could suck my nipples.

'You need to hold me securely in order for me to move as you instruct me to do,' I whispered in his ear.

Wow, I thought, *this lovemaking is truly fantastic!* I had no problem having an orgasm, and I felt Donald ejaculate. So he had no problem enjoying it as well. We were both out of breath and very sweaty by the time we collapsed onto the bed.

'I am speechless,' said Donald. 'You are my very own Lady

Catherine, and I will love and protect you until I die,' he whispered.

Babs prepared a cheese pie for my evening meal and asked me if she could she finish up earlier than normal. I agreed that it would be perfectly all right.

Donald dressed up and hastily left the manor. Someone came and collected him, so very soon, I was on my own, apart from being with my two beautiful dogs.

After eating my evening meal, I settled down in the large lounge. I was cosy, and the fire was blazing high. The two dogs were asleep at my feet.

I decided to try looking in the manor's library for any information about a Lady Catherine or the castle itself. I had looked on the Internet, but I had found nothing of any relevance.

The library was laid out in two sections. I found all the really old journal in the second section, which was situated in a separate room. There was bad smell in that room that indicated age and mould. Most of the ancient books had been stored in special boxes made of acid free, archival-type carboard to help to preserve them.

I spent a long time going along each bookshelf until I finally found a few books that were dated around the time the castle was built. *It's a starting point*, I thought to myself. I took two large old journals into the lounge, poured myself a large whisky, and started to read.

At last, I found some information. The castle had been

built in the latter end of the year 1200 by the McFadden Clan. In 1336, the English defeated the Scots and took over the castle, and the McFaddens fled. As far as I could make out, Lady Catherine, wife of a McFadden, was captured and was left behind.

In the other journal, there was mention of a Lady Catherine who, after being left in the hands of the English, had fallen in love with the head of the English army. He could have been a lord or a knight, but in 1336, there was mention that King Edward III had been in that very same castle. Could it be that the Lady Catherine had fallen in love with King Edward III and that he had fallen in love with her?

The journals detailed the story of the Scots defeating the English a few years later when the castle was re-taken by the McFaddens. Catherine was reunited with her husband, McFadden, but he physically and mentally abused her. Could it be that she missed her English lover and was not prepared to return to her role as the wife of McFadden?

There was just one small paragraph at the end of the second journal, and it read, 'The lady was placed in the castle's dungeon, where she lived, only brought out into the daylight when McFadden needed use of her.'

I wondered if the lady was Lady Catherine. And who had arranged for the tapestry to be woven? Was it the McFaddens, or was it the English? Was Lady Catherine ever rescued by her English lover? So many questions, and such a sad love story.

It was getting late, so I placed the two books on a small

table so that I could show Donald what I had found out. I poured myself one more whisky, and as I turned, to my horror, I saw someone standing in the corner of the room. The dogs immediately jumped up and started growling. Jess was going forward with all her teeth showing. I was terrified. All I could see in the flickering shadows was a man wearing a metal helmet with a nose protector. No sooner had I looked twice than he had gone. The dogs settled back down, but I was left shaking and terrified. I was all on my own in a very large old manor in deepest Scotland. I knew that there were security personnel on patrol outside, but I did not know how to summon them.

I tried to compose myself, but that was not happening. I was truly terrified. It could only have been an apparition … but was it?

I decided that, together with the dogs, I needed to be locked in our bedroom. There, I would wait for Donald to return home.

I called the dogs and ran into the hall. All I could make out was that, instead of the staircase being to the left of me, there was a dark wooden staircase in front of me. I was so disoriented and still terrified. I kept calling the dogs, as I did not want them to leave me. Eventually, I was able to make out the staircase I knew was really there, and I made my way up into our room. I locked the door. I cuddled on the bed with the two dogs. No way was I was going to get undressed. I needed to be dressed in case I had to flee the manor.

I did not know whether I should phone Donald or not, but I decided against that. He was celebrating a stag night, so what could he do?

I must have fallen asleep. I was awakened by Donald banging on the bedroom door. I unlocked the door and flung myself into his arms. I hastily tried to tell him what had happened to me earlier on in the evening. It sounded so ridiculous. I was just so relieved that now Donald would be beside me in bed.

'Shh! Come on, Catherine, calm down now!' whispered Donald. 'You probably fell asleep in the lounge and, with the help of the whisky, you had a really bad dream.'

'It was not a dream! The dogs were ready to protect me,' I said. 'How can you explain why I saw a dark wooden staircase in front of me?'

'Come on, curl up with me. You are shaking. You have got yourself into a state of panic. Tomorrow, you show me the books that you have been reading, and I will show you an explanation for your over-active imagination.'

After a few reassuring kisses, and with his arms holding me tightly, I finally drifted into a heavy sleep. A loud crash and bangs from the ground floor woke us both up. I screamed and grabbed hold of Donald. I held on to him so tightly that he could not move.

'For God's sake, Catherine, let go of me. I can hardly get a breath, let alone move! It is William downstairs. I had to bring him home with me as he was so drunk he didn't know who he was or what he was doing.'

'What was that banging noise?'

'Goodness knows. I suppose I had better go and make sure he's all right,' Donald whispered.

'Don't leave me!' I shouted. 'Don't leave me on my own!'

'Stop this, Catherine! Stay here. I will be back in a moment.' He left me and went down the staircase.

'Catherine!' Donald was shouting. 'I need some help! I need to phone for an ambulance! William has hurt himself. Come here and help me!'

I ran down the staircase and into the lounge. William had fallen against the marble coffee table and cut his forehead. He was totally knocked out. There was blood everywhere. With the help of clean cotton towels, I managed to keep the wound from opening any further. I tried to talk William into coming round, which I thought I had managed to do, but as I placed him into the recovery position, he was sick all over me.

The ambulance was with us in no time at all. William was slowly regaining consciousness, but he had a concussion, and the ambulance took him to the general hospital. Donald arranged for one of his estate employees to drive us to the hospital, as he'd had too much to drink and was not able to drive. I was not prepared to stay in that manor on my own, so I insisted that I also go to the hospital with Donald. Along the way, Donald had to phone Ann, William's bride to be. Boy, was Donald going to be in trouble!

Sure enough, Ann was totally disgusted with Donald and would not give him the time of day. She said she would make her way to the hospital, but she stated that she did not want to see Donald at all.

We arrived at the hospital before Ann, so we waited at William's bedside. His cut was stitched, and he was waiting for blood test results. Nobody was sure how much blood he had lost. William was fine, but Donald was not! He looked as if he was in shock!

As Ann came through the door, shouting and blaming Donald, I retreated to the back of the room and sat down out of firing range. The woman who was with Ann turned to Donald and said, 'The least you could have done was to say you were leaving. I thought you were going to stop all night with me. Have I said or done something wrong?' She then whispered, 'Did you not enjoy me?' But I had heard her words.

Donald immediately said, 'Annette, this is Catherine. She is staying with me at the manor.' I presume that Donald tried to introduce us in the hope that this Annette would not say anything else, but, no, that did not work.

'You bastard, Donald!' she shrieked, and she flew at Donald, trying to hit him. Hospital security was called, and Donald and I made a hasty retreat.

As we returned to Donald's waiting car and driver, Donald turned to me and said, 'Well, tonight went really well, didn't it?'

'In what way?' I asked.

'William will never forget his stag night, will he?'

'I doubt that William will be able to remember anything at all. You are in serious trouble with Ann, and your lover, Annette, will probably never forgive you,' I said sarcastically.

'I don't want a conversation with you. Don't speak to me again tonight!' shouted Donald as we got into the car. I thought it best to stay quiet, and we drove back to the manor in silence.

When we arrived back at the manor, it was early morning, and Babs and the house staff were already at work. Donald explained to Babs what was required in the lounge, mainly, a complete clean to remove all the blood off the furnishings.

'Right!' Donald said to me. 'Show me the two books you say you were reading last night!'

I followed Donald into the lounge, but the two books were not there. 'I left them on the small table over there. I was going to show you what I had found,' I said. 'Someone must have moved them!'

'Who?' he shouted.

'I don't know. Go and see if someone has put them back in the library.'

'Okay. Come on. We will go and have a look.' I hesitated. 'Come on, Catherine. I am very tired, and I can do without all this nonsense.' He was shouting now. He was really bad tempered.

As we entered the old library, I could see that there were no spaces where books were missing. 'Someone must have put them back!' I said quietly.

'Of course,' said Donald very sarcastically. 'This just proves that you returned the books, and on falling asleep, you had a rather disturbing dream. I don't want any more theatricals! I have had a very busy race week down in Cumbria. I drove us both here yesterday, and last night was just hilarious! I am on the verge of exhaustion! I am going to bed now to sleep for a fortnight! If you are going to come, bring us both a hot chocolate!' Donald then pushed passed me and headed up the staircase.

When I returned to our room with two cups of hot chocolate as I had been ordered, Donald was fast asleep. I did not want to disturb him, but I was also very tired and fretful. I gently climbed into the bed, drank my drink, and before long, I too was fast asleep.

We must have both slept all day. Donald woke me by putting his arms around me.

'What time is it?' I asked.

'Time for us to go to bed, I think,' replied Donald. 'It's ten o'clock and pretty dark outside. If I bring you a sandwich and a coffee, can we stop here in bed until the morning?'

'Why not?' I answered thoughtfully. 'It is too late to get up now. I don't want to go downstairs. The staff will all have gone home now.'

'Enough is enough! Don't you dare start spouting off again about your apparitions! Take it from me – you had a bad dream.

Now get over it!' said a very bad tempered Donald.

Donald ran down to the kitchen, so I quickly undressed and jumped into the shower. When he returned, Donald shouted, 'Come on! Hurry up. I have made us a bed picnic.'

When I came out of the shower room, I could not believe my eyes. There, all over the bed, were plates of all sorts of finger foods, from bread sticks to pickles, from cheeses to cooked meats. On the table, there was a large trifle along with dishes and cutlery.

'Wow! We will never eat all this!' I remarked. I had to laugh. It looked as if Donald had emptied the whole fridge.

'I have brought my Lady Catherine a bottle of white wine. I shall be having a bottle of red wine. We must keep up appearances when dining,' Donald said, laughing.

We had a fantastic picnic. We laughed, joked, ate, and drank. When we had finished, we both moved everything off the bed and placed it on the table.

The night was made complete as we made love over and over again. I had forgotten how good Donald was. In fact, I had forgotten how good we were together.

I loved the feel of us both curled up together, our arms wrapped around each other, holding one another so tightly. I did not dare mention the woman, Annette, and I knew that I must never mention what I had seen in the lounge that previous evening.

***

The days leading up to William and Ann's wedding were brilliant. Donald did not have to work, so we spent all our time together.

On our first visit to the stables, Donald asked me to close my eyes as he had a surprise for me. I closed my eyes and waited. I thought that perhaps he had another foal to show me, but no!

'Open your eyes,' Donald said.

There in front of me was Bess! I was so happy that Bess was back with her master.

'Don't forget that you said you would stay with me for three weeks if I brought Bess back here,' Donald said.

'I have not forgotten,' I said, laughing.

We spent quality time together, riding through the woods and fields. We had meals out with Donald's friends. We curled up at night in front of the lounge fire. I had to accept that perhaps I'd actually had a really bad dream.

The day before the wedding, I knew I had to find out what my role was going to be at the wedding. 'You are the best man,' I said to Donald, 'and as such, you will be needed with the wedding party. Where am I to be? Where do I sit in the church? Where do I sit at the reception? How do I get to the church and the reception?' I was a bit nervous.

'I have arranged that you shall have your own car and

chauffeur. He will bring you to the church, and you will sit at the back. From the church, he will take you to the reception where I shall take you to your table. I will be watching you and making sure you are all right all through the wedding meal and speeches. After that, I will be all yours. Does that sound all right?' He had a large grin on his face.

'I want my driver to be in full uniform,' I said, laughing. 'Hat, gloves, and boots!'

'Your wish is my command!' replied Donald.

'If Annette is the chief bridesmaid and you are the best man, why did you need me as a plus one? Surely, you did not need me to come.'

'I wanted you here. Why bring Annette into this conversation?' asked Donald rather angrily. He refused to continue with that conversation!

The night before the wedding, Donald and I were invited to William's home. Donald's car and driver took us and waited for us so we could have a drink.

William's parents made us very welcome, which was more than could be said of Ann and her parents, and of course, the chief bridesmaid, Annette. There was no love lost between Ann and Donald. She blamed him for the very ugly and damaged face of her intended husband, William. It was quite comical though.

Annette never left Donald alone. I was being pushed into the background, but I just continued to be there for Donald.

I knew that they had a history together. I could see it in their eyes. When I started to feel uncomfortable, I asked Donald if it was all right if we returned to the manor. Donald understood and was most apologetic. That night, as we held each other close, Donald wanted to know if there was a chance that one day I would make a stand and fight for his affections. I did not understand what he was asking of me, and to be honest, I did not want to know. I just wanted this damn wedding to be over and done with. I knew that I was not in love with Donald, but I loved him in my way. If I were to decide that I wanted to marry Donald McFadden, I knew that I could make him love me. I knew he was smitten with me now, and as the weeks went by, he had become more and more reliant on me for friendship, sex, affection, and love. We had a very strong sexual bond. Donald had quite a sexual appetite, and when I was staying with him, he never once was interested in other women. The more we enjoyed sex, the more he wanted from me. He was not a selfish lover. He seemed to get more pleasure from pleasing me than from pleasing himself.

What would I do if our relationship took a very serious turn? I could never be lady of the manor. I hated the manor. I was fearful of the manor. Perhaps, with time, as a healer, one day, I would not be frightened in that place.

***

The day of the wedding arrived. Donald had to leave and meet all the other wedding party gentlemen. They were all to be in full Scottish dress. He had explained that my car and chauffeur would bring me to the church and that he would be there, ready to seat me.

The wedding was scheduled for mid-afternoon so that the reception could continue well into the night.

I had plenty of time to prepare myself for a wedding which I really did not want to attend. I had brought to Scotland a beautiful outfit that was perfect for a wedding – a heavy knit silk dress and jacket. The colour was pale blue, but when it moved, it shone pale green. It was exquisite. I accessorized with hair flowers, gloves, shoes, and evening bag, all in a lovely silver-grey colour. My nails were to be painted dark green, and I had chosen all my make-up to match my outfit. I would wear my diamond earrings and a crystal neck choker with matching bracelet and watch.

Once ready, I went to see Babs to see what her reaction was to my wedding outfit. She was quite taken aback at my new look. She was very complimentary and even said that Donald would be so proud of me.

Donald had spent many hours at the table in the lounge, composing his best man's speech while I sat in front of the large fire with my beautiful dogs. Finally, he had left to join the wedding party.

Now it was time to get this day started and finished. Donald's driver, dressed in full chauffeur gear, collected me and took me to the church. Donald came out to greet me. The whole complement of wedding party men looked spectacular in their traditional Scottish garb. Donald looked amazed when he saw me. 'You look beautiful! I feel so proud of you,' he said, and then he escorted me into the church. My car and chauffeur waited for me.

As I sat at the back of the church, I watched all the guests coming in. There were so many women on their own. I knew that Donald must have been interested in at least some of them at some time or other. He was a very famous, wealthy, eligible bachelor. Could it be that I had a chance of securing a future for myself with Squire Donald McFadden? I decided there and then to take my relationship with Donald to another level. I would show other women that they had better keep their distance as Squire Donald McFadden was taken. More to the point, I had to persuade Donald to love me unconditionally.

After the service, as all the guests congregated outside the church, I waited patiently for the wedding photographs to be taken. Donald did not seem to want to leave my side; in fact, he left me only when he was called to have a photograph taken. I looked into his eyes, and the sexual thrill went all through my body. By the look on his face, he was feeling exactly what I was feeling. From that moment, Squire Donald McFadden held onto me and showed everyone there that I was the only woman for him and that he was serious about our relationship.

As Donald had to leave with the wedding party, I was escorted to the castle reception by my chauffeur. Once I arrived, Donald was there to take me to a seat that had been reserved for me at one of the large circular reception tables. I was seated next to Annette's plus one, a man called Michael, who was extremely good company.

The food was excellent. The speeches were really good.

Donald's speech was hilarious. Michael and I could not stop laughing. When the meal came to the end, and the band started to play for the newlyweds' first dance, Donald and Annette took to the dance floor. Annette was dancing so closely to Donald, and I could tell that he was really enjoying it.

Right! I thought. I asked Michael to dance with me, and I held him close … very close. Perhaps, it was not the right thing to do, but the look on Donald's face said it all. He was furious. He was jealous. He was really upset and angry. He walked across the dance floor with Annette in tow and gave Annette to Michael whilst taking hold of me and dancing ever so close to me.

'What are you doing, Catherine?' he whispered.

'Dancing as you were with Annette,' I replied. 'I want you for myself. No other woman is going to dance with you like that!'

'Right! I want you for myself, and no other man is going to dance with you like that!' exclaimed Donald. At which point, we both laughed and kissed right there on the dance floor.

It was now a certainty that Donald and I were an item – lovers, best friends, and partners in a relationship.

That night, when we returned to the manor, we were both so happy and contented. Our day together had been brilliant. Donald had introduced me to everyone. It was a pity that Donald's mother was still in France. I needed to meet her.

We could not wait to go to bed and play with each other.

We made love and held each other close.

Just before we fell asleep, Donald said, 'The Thistle Golf Hotel and Resort opens next weekend. I have offered the castle to the Hague Corporation for their use. They arrive on Wednesday for a week. My estate manager has arranged an entertainment programme for them, which will complement the activities of the opening of the golf resort. I would appreciate your help with this.'

'Of course!' I said, too afraid to ask if Thomas Hague would be there. 'Donald, I have not come prepared to act as a lady of this house, especially if you are to entertain the Hague Corporation. I really need to have the appropriate clothing. Any chance Babs could take me shopping in Edinburgh? She could take me to all the good outdoor clothing stores.'

'You do as you need. I will give you my card, and I will also make arrangements for you to go to my outfitters. I want you to have everything that you wish for and more. And please don't forget the fancy knickers and silk slips.' We both laughed and cuddled.

I lay awake in bed for ages. The thought of Thomas Hague being here in Scotland made me feel sick and also excited. I just hoped and prayed that Thomas Hague was not one of the Hague Corporation guests.

Thomas Hague was always in my thoughts. I did my best to ignore all the thoughts and feelings that I had for him. I had only been with Thomas for a few months in total, but I knew that I loved him so much, and I would do forever and a day.

The next day, Donald and I woke up to the sound of heavy rain.

I opened the curtains in our bedroom and couldn't believe how much rain was pouring down.

We had a leisurely breakfast together and retired to the lounge so Donald could read the Sunday papers. 'I don't think we will be able to go riding today,' he said. 'It seems this weather is in for the foreseeable future. I'm concerned about the birds for the shoot next week. And I'm also concerned about the flooding risk to the river and the fish stock lake. This could be quite serious.'

The heavy rain continued for days. The Hague Corporation party arrived at the castle on the Wednesday and were due to stop a week.

It had been arranged that, on the following Thursday, Donald would take the men from the corporation around the estate. He was to show them the racing stables, the trout rivers, the land and woods that had been prepared for the shoot, and, of course, the manor itself.

On Monday, Babs and I had a full day out in the city shopping for suitable clothes for me, and I made sure I bought some for Donald as well.

I bought some great tweed culottes and beautiful woollen jumpers – all matching, colour-coordinated outfits. I got some tall boots and also some short boots that would suit anything. I looked brilliant in everything that I had purchased.

Since Monday, Donald and all of his male employees had been knee deep in mud and water, trying to keep various areas from becoming dangerously flooded. They'd had to dig trenches around the stables to keep the floodwater out. The river had burst its banks, and all of the bottom fields were under water. Some areas of the woods were completely flooded, and most of the nesting birds had either fled and left their nests or had died.

Villages had been flooded. Tenants had to be relocated to safe accommodations. Roads were inaccessible, and some small stone bridges had been totally destroyed.

On Thursday, the rain was still coming down. There was no way that Donald and the estate manager could entertain the Hague Corporation men by giving them a tour of the estate.

Donald was quite worried. 'This is a real mess,' he said. 'I dread to think what is happening at the golf resort. It must be a complete washout. There will be a considerable amount of damage done just to the course itself. I presume they will cancel the opening now.'

On the Thursday, it was decided that Donald and the estate manager would bring the Hague Corporation men to the manor. They would arrive after lunch, so Babs made small Scottish snacks and biscuits. Brandy glasses were warmed by the large open fire in the lounge. Brandy and whisky were placed on the tables. The large doors to the lounge were opened wide to bring in the vast space of the hall. If the rain stopped, at least Donald could take them to the stables. But it continued to rain.

I told the chamber girls to wear their uniforms – little black dresses and tights with white pinafores and small white hats. I did not have to request that Babs wear her uniform; she was already dressed in it, and beautiful it was. I also dressed up accordingly in outdoor tweeds and long boots to complement the culottes.

A half hour or so after, they had arrived and made themselves comfortable. Then, I made my entrance. Of course, I knew the majority of the men; after all, I had spent an evening with them all in Los Angeles at Mr. and Mrs. Hague's golden wedding celebrations. It was at this grand celebration that I had first met Squire Donald McFadden.

I looked around the room as Donald welcomed me into the proceedings. Thank goodness that I did not see Thomas Hague. I could relax now.

I made my way around the room, talking to the guests individually. As I gave Justin, who was Thomas's brother, a large hug and said I was so pleased to see him, my world stopped as Justin said, 'Thomas is outside, there at the front, having a cigarette.'

I could feel myself shaking. I knew I had to confront him sooner rather than later, so I went out through the front door, taking with me a large umbrella. I could see that he was standing in one of the stone porches at the end of the manor. He had his back to me, but I would have recognized him anywhere.

As it continued to rain, with my umbrella up, I walked to the stone porch. I stood there waiting for him to turn round. My heart was pounding, and I felt quite sick.

Still smoking his cigarette, he turned. We just stood there in silence, looking at each other.

At last, Thomas spoke. 'This is one of the weirdest experiences I have ever encountered. I was looking out over the fields, thinking about you. I was thinking that here I was in Scotland, many miles away from America, and you could be not far away from me in England. I was wondering how far away from here you were and what would you be doing. When I turned around and saw you, I thought I was still daydreaming.' Then, he shouted, 'What the hell are you doing here?'

I calmly said, 'Hello, you!'

'You look good, Catherine!'

'You look good, Thomas!'

'Come here away from the rain.' He beckoned to me.

I walked straight over to him and into his arms. We kissed lightly. All those feelings were still there – the delicious sexual attraction, the desire, the memories, the heartache, and of course, the love we both had for each other. We kissed again, only this time we kissed with purpose – hard, pleasing, sexual kissing.

'What are you doing here? I presume it is something to do with Squire Donald McFadden.'

'Yes. After we met in Los Angeles, we kept in touch. Donald and I have a close relationship, but nothing too serious.'

'You mean you are fucking each other!'

'How dare you make such a crude remark? You know nothing. I have to go in now. It was good to see you again,' I hissed through my teeth.

As I walked away towards the manor door, Thomas said, 'Why do I always have to say—'

But before he could complete his sentence, I completed it for him: 'Catherine, lose the attitude!' We both laughed.

When I returned to the hall and lounge, Donald was not amused and let me know that he was very angry with me. I walked over to him and said, 'I have a great idea. Why don't I set out all the small whisky tasting glasses on the far table and ask Babs to bring a dozen or so whisky bottles from the cellar. She could bring a selection of whiskies from all the local distilleries. Your guests will really enjoy trying all the different blends, and they will become quite happy as they try them.'

Donald agreed that it would be a good idea. 'Were you talking to Thomas Hague outside?' he asked.

'Yes,' I replied. I made no other comment.

Once everything was set up, and our guests were well into the whiskies, I retreated to the kitchen and sat there quietly thinking about Thomas. He came in and sat at the table with me.

'I am sorry. I did not mean to offend you. It is nothing to do with me what you do and who you do it with.' He spoke in a very sarcastic way.

I remained silent. I did not want to speak to him. I felt very fretful, so I had to watch what I said; otherwise, I would have probably burst into tears.

We sat there in silence.

'I want to see you, Catherine!' Thomas finally said. 'Give me your mobile phone number, and I will send you mine. I don't need any foreign codes, as this phone is an English mobile phone. I use it only while I'm here.'

I gave him my mobile number.

'Can you get away to meet me? When and where?' Thomas asked.

'I really don't know. It is so difficult at the moment with this damn weather. How long are you here for?' I replied excitedly.

'Maybe three weeks or so.'

'If I could arrange to go home to England, would you come and see me? I really want to hold you. I want you to make love to me like you used to do,' I whispered slowly, trying not to get emotional.

As Thomas left the kitchen, he said, 'I will contact you. I have missed you too, Catherine.' Then, he was gone.

I got dressed in all my weatherproof clothing and took the dogs for a long walk in the rain. No one could tell that I was crying as the rain ran down my face. I would give anything to have Thomas by my side again. I was so in love with him. I would always be in his debt, but I would also always love him, forever and a day.

When I finally returned to the manor, everyone had left. Babs had finished and gone home to her husband, and the day-time staff had also left.

Babs had baked Donald and I a meat pie for our evening meal. Everything was set out all ready for me to heat up and dish up. I went to retrieve my phone from my shoulder bag, but the phone was missing. I knew I had left it in my shoulder bag, which hung on the coat rails in the kitchen. I looked everywhere for it, just in case it had fallen out onto the floor. It was nowhere to be found. There was only one person who had a reason to take it, and that was Donald.

I walked into the lounge to find Donald, as usual, sitting at the table reading and making notes on his laptop.

'That went so well, did it not? You were a genius, my beautiful Lady Catherine.' He laughed.

'Yes, thank goodness it is over with. Are you ready if I dish out our evening meal?' I said quietly.

'Yes, I'll open a bottle of wine. What's the matter, Catherine?'

'I can't find my mobile phone. I've looked everywhere for it,' I said, and I watched his reaction.

'It will turn up. And if it doesn't, I will buy you another one. Is that okay? Does that make you feel better?'

'Not really,' I said, and for the rest of the evening, I curled up with the dogs and ignored Donald.

In bed that night, all I could think about was the fact that Thomas could not contact me now. I was angry with Donald; I knew that he had taken my phone.

Donald put his arms around me and hugged me. 'The entertainment will be really good tomorrow night at the castle. My estate manager has arranged for some excellent professional acts for the themed Scottish night. I'm looking forward to it, and I hope you are as well. I have to dress up again in all my Scottish finery, and so do all the other Scottish men. Should be really good.'

'Donald, when am I to go home? Would it not be best for you to take me when you have to go to your Lancastrian estate? I presume that is soon, as you have not been for a few weeks.'

'Not going to happen, Catherine! Too much to do here now. Why do you want to go home? Am I missing something here? Is this because you have seen Thomas Hague? From now on, I do not want you to have anything to do with him. You will not talk to him, and at the castle tomorrow night, you will not dance with him. Do I make myself clear?' I did not respond. 'I said, do I make myself clear?' shouted Donald.

I thought it best to keep quiet, and I drifted into sleep.

The following morning, the weather hadn't changed: rain, rain, and more rain. Donald was out early checking on the stables and was very concerned when he returned to the manor.

'I've been to Mother's cottage to make sure everything is all right, and of course it is, but I am afraid the access road has been badly damaged. Mother says that she and Peter are on their way home from France. It looks as if they will be staying here at the manor until such time as the access road can be repaired. I am not looking forward to that!' He sounded weary.

We were both looking forward to the Scottish evening at the castle. Even though we were both ready in good time, Donald's phone never stopped, and of course, he had to answer all his incoming calls. It was one emergency after another.

We arrived at the castle a little late, but we made our way around the room, greeting everyone at all the tables. I had a small conversation with Susan. She still looked the same, and Justin's wife looked the same. Donald and I had already met Justin and Thomas the previous day at the manor.

Finally, we were seated at our table, and we could relax at last. Most of Donald's staff who were not working that night had been invited to the event. Even the manor's staff – Babs and her husband and even the chamber girls and their partners – were there.

An hour or so into the festivities, Donald received a phone call. He jumped up, called for all his staff, and they all raced out of the castle hall. I ran after them. 'Catherine!' Donald shouted when we reached the entryway. 'The stable roof is coming down. I'll have to move all the horses to different farms. I'll send a car back for you to take you back to the manor.' He turned to leave.

I shouted to him that I did not want to be at the manor on my own, especially at night.

'See if there are any rooms left here at the castle. If there are, take one, and I'll send a car for you in the morning.'

Just as his ride arrived, I realized that I was more afraid of being in a compromising situation with Thomas here at the castle than I was of any ghostly apparition at the manor. I shouted to Donald, 'I'll stay at the manor. Can you send a car for me later?'

'Correct decision!' shouted Donald through the rain.

I returned to my seat as the entertainment continued. During the refreshment interlude, Thomas came and sat with me. He was concerned to have seen Donald and some of his workforce leaving the castle. I explained the situation to him, and I told him that I had turned down a room at the castle because I would have definitely wanted Thomas to stay with me and have sex with me. We both laughed because we both knew that is what would have happened. I also told Thomas that I thought Donald had taken my phone.

'I have left a couple of messages for you. Sorry that you will have to sort that out. How can I contact you now? I have to see you. What can we do?' asked Thomas.

At the end of the night, the master of ceremonies played dance music. Thomas and I danced, holding each other close.

'I can taste you. I can smell you. I am constantly thinking of you. What are we to do, Catherine? There must be a way of sorting this mess out,' said Thomas.

'Make a move, Thomas, just make a move. I cannot do it for you. I will be there by your side when you do. I need you, Thomas. I don't want to drift through life without you. Please make a move to leave Susan,' I pleaded.

'Catherine, your car is here!' someone shouted. I collected my things and left the castle.

I was fine at the manor. I went straight to bed and took my lovely four-legged friends with me. Poor Donald. He had worked so hard over the last few days. I knew that he would be absolutely exhausted when he finally came back to the manor. It was about eight in the morning when Donald finally climbed into bed. As he got into bed, I was getting up and out of bed. We had a cuddle and a laugh at the situation.

'I really love you, Catherine,' whispered Donald. 'I need to talk to you.'

'You can talk to me later. You need to sleep now. Do you want me to wake you this afternoon with a surprise?' I whispered.

'You dirty mare!' Donald laughed.

As I finished my breakfast in the kitchen, Babs came in and announced that I had visitors – Justin and Thomas Hague. She had taken them into the lounge.

As I walked in the lounge, Justin walked out of the room, closing the door behind him.

'I needed to see you on our own,' said Thomas. 'We are setting off back to America today. The entire opening and the tournaments have been cancelled. It's all a complete washout. I just wanted to say goodbye in person.'

'Well, that was thoughtful of you! You needn't have bothered. I could not care less about what you want! Just go, Thomas. This will be the last time that you hurt me. I wish I had never met you!' I tried not to break down.

'Catherine, come here. I need to hold you. I really love you, but it will never work out for us. Just let me hold you!' As he held me, he broke down and cried.

I just stood there holding him tightly. I had nothing to say. It had all been said before. Justin opened the lounge door, and Thomas left. I heard their car drive away.

It was still raining, but not as hard as it had been. I put on my outdoor gear, collected the dogs, and went for a long walk. I could not think. It was as if my brain had suddenly stopped working. I just wanted to go home. I really disliked the manor. I loved Donald in my own way. At least Donald was honest with me, and he loved me in his own way.

I made my way back to the manor. The dogs were wet through, and so was I. As I entered the kitchen from the back entrance, I encountered a woman and a man. They were sitting at the table having some of Babs's homemade soup. I immediately knew who they were.

'Mrs. McFadden, I presume,' I said quietly.

'Yes,' she said. 'You must be Catherine. This is my partner, Peter.' She looked at me up and down.

'Has Donald informed you that we are to move back into the manor until the access road to our cottage has been repaired?' she asked.

'Yes, he has,' I politely answered.

'Mrs. Bumble has prepared a room for us. What room are you in, Catherine?' Mrs. McFadden asked.

I saw Babs put her hands up to her mouth with surprise. 'Donald's room,' I answered.

The look on Donald's mother's face was one of disbelief. 'You and Donald are more than just good friends then!' she hissed at me.

I nodded agreement and ran out of the room in order to wake Donald and tell him that his mother and Peter had arrived.

I jumped into bed with Donald and curled up in his arms. 'Your mother and Peter are in the kitchen. I don't think she has taken to me. Perhaps it would be better if you and I live in this bedroom for … like … forever!' I said, laughing. 'Come on get up now, and sort your mother out.'

'Wait, Catherine. I need to talk to you before we go downstairs,'

'No, come on. I am not going downstairs without you, and I want to have lunch with you,' I insisted.

I ran down to the kitchen and asked Babs to prepare Donald and me some of her soup. She gave me my phone, saying that she had found it on the window ledge in the kitchen porch. The battery was dead. Could it be that Donald had not taken it after all? I could quite easily have left it there. Just then Mrs. McFadden called me into the lounge.

'I presume Donald has told you that he will be moving back into The Gables on a more permanent basis. It was decided some time ago that, when Donald was ready to move back into The Gables, Sheila would be moving in with him. They would give it a go. They never had much of a chance before, but circumstances today will help them sort themselves out. Don't you think?'

As I was trying to digest what she had just said, Donald walked into the lounge.

'You have not told her, have you?' said Mrs. McFadden.

'My name is Catherine, and no, Donald has not told me that he plans to move in with Sheila,' I said as I turned to leave the lounge.

'Wait! Catherine, wait! I needed to talk to you. It is not what it seems. I do not want to lose you!' said Donald.

'You just have!' I said quietly.

'Listen, I have to go out to one of the farms. I'll be back in a couple of hours. I will sort this out. It is not what it seems to be.' And then he left.

I went into the kitchen and said to Babs, 'How long have you known that this was going to happen?'

'A week or so,' Babs replied. 'It was not up to me to say anything.'

'Please phone me a taxi and tell me when it arrives!'

There was no way I was going to stay in the manor for a second more than I had to do. I was angry, not upset. I was very angry and disappointed with Donald. I really thought that he respected me and loved me in his own way. How wrong I had been – again! What was the matter with me? It seemed that no one I loved wanted to take a chance on me!

I wasted no time in packing all my belongings back into my suitcase. As far as I was concerned, Donald could keep all my new outfits. Perhaps he could give them away to the needy, as I had no use for them.

By the time I had thrown all my things into my suitcase, the taxi had arrived. I made a hasty retreat into the taxi, and we drove away. I did not say goodbye to anyone, not even Babs. I instructed the taxi to take me to the Edinburgh railway station. When I arrived, I was in luck – there was a train that stopped at Lancaster, and I had to wait only an hour for it.

I settled down on the train and tried to compose my thoughts. The anger I felt changed to upset and heartache. How could Donald do this to me? I really thought we had something good going for us. I had also once thought that Thomas and I had something good going for us. How wrong could I be –

twice? I now felt so defeated. I had no idea what I was to do or where I was to go. Perhaps I should sell up and move away. Make a fresh start. My son was away travelling. My daughter, Carol, had settled down with her boyfriend and would probably be getting married soon. And my daughter, Jennifer, had found herself a position in Spain as a translator. My children had sorted their futures out. Why could I not secure a future that would make me happy? I felt so lost, and of course, I felt sorry for myself. To finish everything off, my phone was dead!

Before long, I was back at home. I was relieved to be secure in my own house. I did not need anyone else. I was soon unpacked. The washing machine was working away, and I was curled up alone in my bed. I was so tired and weary that I thought I might sleep for days.

The next morning, I woke up to sunshine and the sound of the birds singing. *No rain down here,* I thought to myself. I was feeling calm, and I did not seem too upset. I was more upset with Thomas. I really loved him, and I wanted to be with him forever. As far as Donald was concerned, I couldn't give a damn! I had put my phone on charge before I went to sleep, so I hastily went to read my messages now that it was fully charged.

Thomas had sent me his mobile number, but it was only for his English mobile. He had left me two other messages as well. The first one was, 'We have to meet up, Catherine. Call Me!' And the second was, 'Still waiting for you to call. I miss you!'

I read those messages over and over again. What would

have happened if I had not lost my phone? Would we have got together? Who knew? I would never know now. All I did know was that, in the end, he did not want me. He was not prepared to give up his lifestyle and his career for me. Twice, he had left me for his lifestyle, and both times, I had ended up heartbroken. *Enough is enough!*

It was good to meet up with my friends, Sarah, Judith, and Elizabeth. I enjoyed meeting them for meals. I was back at the golf club, enjoying the social aspect of the place. I also agreed to go on holiday with them. They had chosen Portugal, and the trip could not have come at a better time for me. They had booked a two-week, all-inclusive holiday. We were to leave in several weeks' time. They had no trouble adding me onto their booking. After all the rain I had encountered, the thought of sand, sea, and sunshine was brilliant.

It was the night before we were to set off to Portugal that Donald appeared on my front door step. As I answered my door, he just stood there, smiling and smoking. He looked so good. He did not speak, so I did not speak. I left the door open, and I returned to my packing. He eventually followed me in. I tried to act as if I was not bothered about him, but I found myself feeling rather flustered – very nervous. He walked over to me and stopped me from continuing with my packing. He pulled me towards him and held me close. He gently brushed my lips with his. Wow! There was such a sexual spark that it took my breath away. I waited as he rubbed his face against my face, cheek to cheek. Wow! The sexual thrill went all over my body. I was embarrassed. I did not want to feel those feelings. I put my arms around his neck. I kissed him, and he kissed me back.

It was not long before he was taking my clothes off, and I was helping him take his clothes off. Not one word was spoken. There was no need to say anything. I wanted Donald to fuck me, and he wanted to fuck me. On the floor, in my lounge, in the midst of all my clothes, which I was supposed to be packing into my suitcase, we lay down naked. I loved the feel of his hands stroking my body. I loved the feel of him holding my breasts and feeling my nipples. I ran my fingers through his hair, holding him so close to me. We were both so sexually excited that nothing would stop us from having sex. I felt him inside me, and he moved with such precision. I had a tremendous orgasm. I felt Donald ejaculate, and we both lay there, trying to catch our breath. It was fantastic.

Eventually, Donald said, 'I only came to have a cup of coffee with you,' and we both laughed.

'Donald, you were brilliant! I had forgotten what a good lover you are.'

'Catherine, you were brilliant. I have never forgotten what a great lover you are!' We both laughed and held each other close for quite a while.

'Where are you going?' asked Donald.

'Portugal for two weeks.'

'When you return, will you seriously consider coming back to me? I have missed you so much.'

'If I did, Donald, there would have to be some dramatic changes to our relationship. Are you prepared to tell Sheila about us and make some commitment to our future together? If you are not, then I don't want to know. Your family and your clan will not approve of me, so you had better think long and hard if you really want me to come back to you!'

'I will if you will!' Donald laughed.

'What does that mean?' I shouted.

'I will see you when you get back from Portugal. Every night, I shall send you a word to make you smile and remember me.' He continued to laugh.

'Go to hell, Donald. I don't want to talk to you anymore. Why did you come here today? I feel as if I am becoming one of your clucking hens. That is the last time I will be used!' I said angrily.

'If you have been used today, then you have used me today as well!' Donald whispered in my ear.

Donald walked out of the front door and drove away. I was so angry with myself. Why had I not been stronger in telling Donald to go and leave me alone? Why had I let him have sex with me?

***

At last, we were in Portugal. I was determined to have a good holiday – plenty of rest, good food and drink, sunshine, and warmth. The resort was magnificent, and the hotel was perfect for us girls.

The first night was really entertaining, and true to his word, Donald texted me a word. The word was *love*. As the two weeks went by, I received a single word every night. Some of the words were innocent, but some of the words were naughty: *Sex. Lips. Orgasm. Tongue. Hands. Erection. Kiss. Stroke. Lick. Bite. Nipples. Sweat. Marriage.*

I must admit, the nightly words made me smile. Why *marriage* for his last word? Was he just being cruel? The problem with Donald was that he was cruel, crude, rude, obnoxious, and spoilt – always having his own way in everything he did, in both work and pleasure.

When I returned home after the holiday, I did not expect to see Donald any time soon, but he surprised me by turning up at my house the day after I arrived at home.

He seemed genuinely pleased to see me. As he constantly tried to get hold of me, I constantly tried to avoid any physical contact with him. Eventually, he sat on one of the sofas in the lounge and said, 'Right. I give in! You are wearing me down! Are we going to get to love one another, or are you going to keep avoiding me all night?'

'Tell me what you want from me, and I will tell you what I want from you,' I said calmly and slowly.

'Are we playing a game?'

'No, I am not playing any more, Donald. I have had enough. I want to move on. So please tell me what you want from me, and I will tell you what I want from you.'

'Okay … I want to marry you. I want to sell The Gables. We should buy a large farmhouse. I mean a really large farmhouse. You can bring the dogs, Jeremy and Jess, and I will build large stables, just for our own horses. We can bring Bess with us. I can concentrate on the breeding program at larger stables somewhere on the estate … do you want me to continue?' He had a large smile on his face.

I was so shocked that I could not think straight. Was he being cruel and just saying those things, or had he really proposed marriage to me?

'Well? Your turn,' said Donald, still smiling at me. 'What do you want from me? You have gone rather quiet. Have I missed something?'

'Yes, you have missed something. You have not told me that you love me,' I whispered.

'Oh! I love you, Catherine Riding. Will you become Catherine McFadden by marrying me?' whispered Donald.

'Yes, I love you, Donald McFadden. If you are really serious, then we have quite a journey to go on together.'

Then we retired to bed and loved each other all night.

***

As the days went by, I was able to understand the overall picture as to how and when Donald was going to put his master plan in place. To start with, he was going to take me to Gretna Green in the last week of December. We would have to stay there for a few days in order to obtain a wedding licence. We would be married by the New Year. Once married, we could tell everyone about our marriage, and then no one could do anything about it. As Donald said, 'To hell with the clan, my mother, Sheila, and her family. In fact, anyone who has an objection to us can just go to hell!'

The key to our future plans was that we had to get married. Donald booked a hotel in Gretna Green, and he booked the registry office for 30 December. There would be no formal honeymoon, as there was plenty of time for that in the future.

Donald and I would live together at my house until such time as Donald could sell The Gables. He already had his larger stables on the Lancastrian estate. He did promise me that, nearer the time of our wedding, he would tell Sheila that he did not love her and that he wanted to start a new life with me. As it was, he was never away from my house. He practically lived there most of the time. Why Sheila did not walk away from him, I will never know.

On the days and nights that Donald stayed at The Gables, I always felt unsure and insecure. I had a feeling that one day, he might let me down and break my heart.

On one such occasion, Donald was to stay at The Gables for a few days because he was to take delivery of certain medicines for the racehorses and certain medical items that were to help with his breeding program. I knew that he would be in Sheila's bed. I did not like the idea at all, but I was not in a good position to start being awkward with Donald.

Chapter 10
Decision Time

It was during this time that I started thinking about Thomas Hague. Recently, Thomas had been in my thoughts and in my heart. I knew that I was never going to be really happy and contented with Donald. I really did not know what to do.

One night, when Donald was staying at The Gables, I found Thomas Hague's website. Just reading about him made me feel as if something was missing for me. There were no contact details on his website, so I wondered if there was a way for me to find a telephone number for him or at least maybe an e-mail address.

I started by contacting the offices at the new golf resort in Scotland. I asked if there was any way that they could pass a message on for me to either Justin or Thomas Hague in America. The person I managed to speak to there said he had no idea how to contact their head office in America, so that was a waste of time. I asked if they had an e-mail address for any of the Hague Corporation's offices in America, and again, I received nothing.

On the Internet, I managed to find the address and telephone numbers of the Hague Corporation in Los Angeles.

The following day, at about lunchtime, I started my quest to try to get a message to Thomas Hague. My message was short and to the point. My message to the Hague Corporation Offices was: 'Would Mr. Justin Hague or Thomas Hague please contact Catherine Riding on this telephone number or by this e-mail address. It is a matter of importance.'

None of the people I managed to speak to on the phone knew how to pass the messages on. I did manage to obtain some useful e-mail addresses, but I was under the impression that no one wanted to accept the responsibility for taking messages from a suspected stalker or a person who might be a security risk.

I made a note of the e-mail addresses I had acquired, and I thought that I would try sending messages at a later date. I had spent so much time on the phone that I had practically given up all hope of trying to contact Thomas. *I will try another day,* I thought to myself.

***

A day or so later, when Donald returned to my house, I decided that I was not going to sit, wait, and fester with the situation that Donald had placed me in.

He was so pleased to be back with me, and he even offered to cook my evening meal. I knew that he had only offered to do that because he found my cooking awful! We had a really good evening, and as usual, we loved each other's company.

As we sat by the warm fire in the lounge, Donald was reading his newspapers, and I was listening to music. I knew that I had to approach the subject of his relationship with Sheila.

'Donald, I need to talk to you about something that is pretty serious to me,' I said quietly.

Donald looked up at me, and as if he knew what I was going to say, responded in the offensive straight away and said, 'What?'

'When you stay at The Gables, do you sleep with Sheila?' Again, I spoke very quietly.

'No! We have separate bedrooms. Do you mean do we have sex?' He was angry now.

'You know what I mean. I want some truthful answers. I need to know!' I said, talking through my teeth.

'Why?' said Donald. 'The last thing I want is to come here and be questioned like a naughty schoolboy. You know how I feel about you, and that should be enough until such time that we are married. I will never hurt you, you know that, so why all the theatricals?'

'I need to know … what is your relationship with Sheila? If you have any respect and feelings for her, you have to tell her that you and she have no future together! Give her a chance to make some life-changing decisions. Surely she knows that you are always staying here with me? She must know that we are lovers? What I want to know is, are you and Sheila lovers?' I stopped there. I wanted to ask him so many questions, but I was becoming quite emotional inside.

Donald looked so angry. 'I am not going to discuss this with you. If I lie to you, I shall find myself in trouble with you, and if I tell you half the truth, I shall find myself in trouble with you, and if I tell you the whole truth and nothing but the truth … well, I am in very serious trouble. I am damned if I do and damned if I don't!' Donald then started to laugh.

By this time, I was extremely angry with him. He was a man who was obnoxious, rude, crude, and very cruel. I was not prepared to be put on any more. Sheila might be prepared to carry on as things were, but I was not. I was not one of his clucky hens. I was not one of his lady playmates. I was supposed to be his future wife.

'Do you have sex with Sheila when you stay at The Gables? I want an answer, Donald. Do you enjoy sex with Sheila? Answer me, Donald! If you deliberately ignore my questions, then, I swear, one day, I will ask Sheila myself!' I knew I had gone too far asking those kinds of questions.

'I have had enough! I am going for a drink. I will probably get drunk, so I don't know if I will be back here tonight!' And after saying that, he stormed out, and I heard him driving away. Ouch!

As soon as Donald had left, I decided to send the e-mails that I had promised myself. I had three e-mail addresses for the Hague Corporation. I worded the e-mails like this: 'For the attention of Mr. Justin Hague and/or Thomas Hague. Please contact Catherine Riding as a matter of importance.' I provided my e-mail and phone contact information.

I had no idea what I would say if Thomas contacted me. All I knew was that we both loved one another and had loved one another for years. Surely that counted for something. I did not want to give up on him. I just needed a way of putting things right.

I was relieved that I had sent the e-mails. Now, all I could do was wait and see. If I did not get a response, then at least I had tried, and communication was not meant to be.

Donald did not phone or text me that night. In fact, I did not hear from him for a couple of days. I made no effort to contact him. I was still upset and angry with him – nothing new there, then!

When Donald finally came to see me, he was very quiet. He was not angry or bad tempered as I expected him to be.

'Can I come in, or are you going to get on my case again? Because if you are, I am leaving now!' said a very meek Donald.

'Please yourself. I really don't care, Donald, what you do!'

'Come here!' he demanded. 'I want to hold you. I really

can't do without you in my life, and I am now frightened that you are changing your mind about us and our future together.' He got hold of me and held me close.

I was so relieved to feel him holding me, giving me those delicious feelings all over. I just held onto him. Now was not the time for me to be awkward with him. We kissed, and Donald insisted that we cuddle up in bed. I had no objections to that.

As we lay together in bed after we had loved each other, Donald answered his mobile phone. 'Mother, how are you?' And straight away, he put his phone on speaker so I could hear their conversation.

'When are you thinking of coming down here?' asked Donald. 'Before I forget, I want you to go into my room. In the bottom of one of my wardrobes, you will find a box with all Catherine's riding gear in it. Can you bring that box with you?'

'Are you still seeing her? What about Sheila?' Donald's Mother asked.

'Of course, I am still seeing Catherine. Nothing will ever part us now. I will be telling Sheila that I am in love with Catherine and that there will be no future for us. I will tell her it would be best if she told her parents and left The Gables when she is sorted and ready to move out.'

'So where are you now?' Donald's mother angrily asked.

'I am in bed with Catherine at her house.'

'Stop fooling about and get yourself sorted!'

'Say hello to Mother, Catherine.'

Donald laughed, and I said, 'Hello, Mrs. McFadden.' The phone line went dead, and we both laughed and cuddled each other.

'Well! Does that make you feel better, listening to what I had to say to Mother?' Donald asked, pulling me closer to him.

'Of course, it does. I really need your reassurances. You still have not answered my questions about you and Sheila, however.'

'That is all you are getting from me!' Donald laughed again.

***

Donald did tell Sheila about us and gave her time to sort herself out. In the meantime, he lived with me, but that did not stop him from going out with his man mates and womanizing.

After three weeks, I had not had a reply from my e-mails to Thomas and his brother. I was convinced that Thomas would have received at least one e-mail and had decided to ignore them and had, as before, decided to destroy my contact information.

Just out of curiosity, I looked on an airline booking site. I found a return flight to Los Angeles that was an absolute bargain. The downside to the price was that it was for the next day. The return flight could be booked as an open ticket. The more I read the details, the more I was convinced that I should just book it and go. At least I could try and find Thomas. After a moment of madness, I had booked and paid for the return flight. Nothing at all could stop me. I booked a room at a Holiday Inn Hotel in North Los Angeles.

I had only a few hours to prepare and pack. I did not tell anyone about my intentions. Early the next morning, I was on my way to the airport. Before long, I was on the flight, and as I settled down in my seat, I wondered what I was to do once I arrived there. I did not feel nervous at all, and I settled down to something to eat and a good sleep.

***

As I walked out of the airport at Los Angeles, I decided against a hire car. I hailed a taxi and gave the driver the name and address of the hotel I had booked online. I also asked the driver all about the Hague Corporation. I asked him if he knew where their offices where. I knew there were more than one block of offices for the Hague Corporation. Nothing made any sense to me, but I had the address of the Hague Corporation headquarters. I made my way there the following day.

On a beautiful day, I set off in a taxi to the Hague headquarters. Once there, I walked through security into a lobby, but I was not allowed to go any further without some details of an appointment that was registered in their system. I also had to register all my passport details, and I had to be interviewed by a security officer. I was told to leave, as they were not prepared to give me any information as to where I could locate

Thomas Hague.

As I was leaving, I happened to overhear a conversation about an important document addressed to Thomas Hague that had to be taken across town to the offices of Turner's Importers, and I then knew exactly where to find Thomas. Susan's surname was Turner.It would seem that Thomas could be working for Mr. Turner, Susan's father. I hailed a taxi, giving my destination as the offices of the Turner Importers, and before long, I was standing outside the offices where Thomas was presumely working.

I knew it was going to be difficult to get into the offices and speak to Thomas. I hastily wrote a note on a piece of paper I had in my bag: 'I am here at these offices. Please do not ignore me. I just want to talk to you. Catherine X.' I then placed the note in my passport and made my way through the large glass entrance doors.

Within seconds, I was stopped and challenged as to what was my business in the Offices. I explained my business and gave the security guard my passport and note, and I asked him to make sure they were given to Mr. Thomas Hague himself.

Obviously, I was not going to be admitted to see Thomas, so I asked the security officer to at least speak to Thomas Hague about my passport and note before he asked me to leave the building. I told him that it was most important and hinted that my message had something to do with a very dear relative. I was taken to a room, and a woman officer stayed with me.

I was waiting for ages. I was so nervous. A gentleman came

into the room and started to interview me. I had to produce my passport. He kept asking me my reason for wanting to see Thomas Hague. I insisted that I would speak only to the Thomas himself. I was starting to get a little frightened, so I insisted that they take my note and my passport and give them to Thomas Hague.

The gentleman took my note and my passport and left me with the female officer. It was ages before he returned. 'Come with me,' he said, and he took me into what I presume were Thomas' offices. I stood there with the gentleman feeling so nervous and sick. Finally, Thomas entered the room.

'You can leave us now,' said Thomas to the man. When we were on our own, he shouted angrily, 'What the hell are you doing here?'

'Hello to you too. Yes, I am fine. How are you?' I said very sarcastically.

'Don't get funny with me! What the hell are you doing here? Who have you come with and why?' He was very angry.

'I wanted to see you and talk to you. I know that you must have received my messages, and you chose to ignore them. Well, guess what? Here I am!' I hissed the words at him.

'Well, talk to me. What do you want?' Thomas said. I had never seen him so angry.

'Forget it! I don't want to talk to you now! I am leaving. Don't worry … you will not see me again. I will be flying home on the next available flight. Good riddance to you!' I was still hissing my words, and I started to leave.

'Where are you staying?' Thomas asked.

I stayed silent. I could not answer. The emotion of seeing him and the way he was treating me had hurt me so much that I was afraid that I was going to let myself down and burst into tears.

'I asked you… where are you staying? Who have you come with?' asked Thomas again.

'Go to hell, and let me leave,' I retorted.

'Calm down! You can't just turn up like this,' Thomas said, still looking very angry.

'I just did! I came on my own, and I have booked into a hotel in North Los Angeles,' I said very quietly. I was feeling so defeated and sick.

Thomas took his phone out, phoned a hotel, and made a booking for me. 'This hotel is nearer these offices. Go and check out of the hotel you are in now and make your way to this hotel. I will see you later tonight.' Thomas handed me a piece of paper with the hotel's details on it. He then asked a security officer to show me out. As I was leaving, Thomas said, 'I have your passport, Catherine, so don't be clever. You had better be at this hotel tonight!'

The security officer escorted me out of the building. I just stood there outside the offices, wondering what to do next. I had not expected Thomas to react to me as he had. Had I been living a lie all these years? Thomas had been wonderful to me in Vegas and again at Scotland. What had changed? I hailed a taxi and returned to the hotel I had booked in North LA.

If Thomas had not kept my passport, I would have definitely returned to the airport and booked the first available flight back home. As it was, I had no option but to move to the hotel that Thomas had booked.

There was no rush to go to the other hotel, so I took my time packing all my things into my suitcase. I showered and dressed in my best clothes. I wore stockings and a suspender belt, a beautiful, long, colourful silk under slip, and a cream cotton shirtdress that buttoned all the way down the front. I wore matching shoes and cream leather bangles on both arms. After I had completed my make-up, I was happy with my appearance. If I was going to be seduced by Thomas, or if I was going to seduce Thomas, I was definitely wearing the correct outfit.

I checked out of the hotel and ordered a taxi to take me to the hotel address that Thomas had written down.

The Sheridan Hotel was just around the corner from the offices, just as Thomas said it would be. At reception, they were aware that I was coming and showed me to a beautiful, large bedroom suite. In the room, apart from a large king-sized bed, there was a large sofa with a coffee table, along with a dining table with four dining chairs. There was a large shower room with all the amenities.

I did not bother to unpack. I realized that I might just end up going back to the airport for a return flight home sooner than I thought I would be.

It was such a long afternoon, waiting for Thomas to turn up. I lay on the bed and tried to sleep. I was so tired and weary.

At last, I heard a knock at the door. I opened the door to Thomas. He still looked angry, and he acted so cold to me. I was shocked. Just looking at him had made my heart beat loud and fast. I looked directly into his eyes. Those delicious sexual feelings were all over my body. There was no denying that the desire I felt for him was tremendous. Why was Thomas not responding to me? We were both silent. Neither of us said a word. Still looking into his beautiful dark eyes, I made a move to get closer to him, and to my horror, he moved away from me.

That was the final straw. What was happening here? I had nothing to lose, so I decided I would try to seduce him. I needed to know if he still desired me and still had feelings for me.

I slowly started to unbutton my dress. When all the buttons were undone, I took the dress off the way I would take a coat off.

'What are you doing, Catherine? You seem to think this is one hell of a game. I still want to know what you are doing here! Save your games as I have to leave to keep an appointment.' This was one angry man.

I ignored what he was saying. I took my shoes off. I took my slip off. I took my knickers off. I left my suspenders and stockings on. I stood against the back wall of the bedroom with one leg slightly raised and resting on the small bedside cabinet. I looked directly into his eyes. He did not ask me to stop. I stroked my breasts and held my nipples. Then, I stroked my body all the way down to my groin area and then between my legs. I then started to stroke myself all the way back up to my breasts, and I finished by holding and squeezing my nipples.

Thomas never moved. He watched every move I made and still managed to keep eye contact with me.

'I have started. Will you finish me?' I said with a large smile on my face.

Within a second, Thomas's clothes were coming off. He discarded them on the floor. With his naked body, he pushed me hard against the wall. He pressed his lips onto mine with such an urgency. Thomas's hands were all over me. He raised my already slightly raised leg further. I felt the penetration. He felt wonderful. The thrills he gave me made it so easy for me to have a powerful orgasm. I was aware of Thomas coming; I could even feel his ejaculation. That sex was so fantastic, not only for me, but I knew that it was also fantastic for Thomas.

We fell onto the bed, wrapped ourselves up in a sheet, and held each other so close. 'Don't let go of me, Thomas! I need to feel you holding me tight,' I whispered.

'Catherine, you know that I really love you, but I cannot have you just turning up here like this. I suffered a terrible depression when you left me first time. It took me such a long time to get over the depression,' whispered Thomas.

'I did not leave you! You threw me out!' I retaliated.

'You chose to leave me! Anyway, every time we meet and then part, I am left with a terrible sadness, and I am not prepared to keep putting myself through it, time after time. I wanted the security of knowing that we had decided to go our own ways and that I would never see you again, but you had different ideas.'

'I shall be on a plane home tomorrow. I promise you that you will never see me again. It was a bad idea coming here to see you. I know that now. If you had been decent and phoned my contact number, I would never have flown here to see you. I know that you must have received at least one of my e-mail messages.' I felt rather fretful.

'Well, you are here now. I suggest that we take off and have a few days together before you return home. I will take you to Santa Barbara, where my boat is. It is beautiful down there. It will be just the two of us, as we used to do. I promise that I will put my arms around you and hold you tight every night! What do you say?' asked Thomas.

'To be honest, I would rather go home now rather than have a few days with you and then have to go home. I miss you every day, and if I spend time alone with you, I will be heart-broken when I have to say goodbye forever,' I whispered, trying not to show how upset I was.

'I have your passport, so I will not take no as your answer. Right. Get dressed. I am going to take you to a lovely restaurant, and we shall enjoy a good meal!' instructed Thomas.

I quickly showered and dressed. I put my warm coat over my dress, and once Thomas was fully dressed and had his coat on, we made our way to the restaurant. We had to walk through a small park area. Thomas offered me his arm, and I hugged his arm, and we talked and laughed and kissed as lovers do, all the way to the restaurant.

Once there, we made ourselves comfortable in what looked like booths. It was similar to a steak house but seemed to have such a brilliant, varied menu. I was not hungry at all, but Thomas said that he had not eaten all day, so he was preparing to enjoy a good meal. Thomas ordered the food, and I warned him that I would not be eating much, but I promised him that I would try and eat something.

As we waited for our food, Thomas held my hand on the table. He was playing with my engagement ring, the one that he had given to me a long time ago.

'Do you wear this ring all the time, or have you just put it on because you might see me?' he asked.

'I wear it all the time. Every day, I look at it and think of you. When Tony brought it to me, I felt so lost and lonely inside. I never got over you asking me to leave!'

'What are we doing, Catherine?' asked Thomas quietly.

Just then, a man came to our table. He was angry with Thomas. He banged his fist on our table and said, 'You are a bastard, Thomas. All those people turned up tonight for you, but you could not be bothered to turn up, and here you are with another bitch!'

'Get lost, Paul. I will talk to you when you are sober!' Thomas was quite angry.

This Paul turned to me and said, 'Do you know where this bastard was supposed to be tonight? He was supposed to be at the dress rehearsal for the wedding at the church. People turned up for him, but he has let everyone down!'

'That is my fault—'

But before I could explain anything, Paul continued. 'Have you met my sister, Susan? Does she know what you and Hague are up to? If she doesn't know, she will know when I go and see her tonight! You won't get away with this, Hague, you bastard.'

'Get lost, Paul!' shouted Thomas. Paul turned and walked away, joining his friends at a table round the corner from where we sat.

While all this unpleasantness was going on, Thomas never removed his hand from my hand on the table. I knew that Thomas was in love with me. He did not care about anyone else, just me.

The food arrived, and I just picked at it. I really was not hungry.

'Are you going to tell me what you wanted to see me about?' asked Thomas as he was eating his meal.

'It doesn't matter now. I made a wrong decision coming all this way. I should have known better. I just want to go home now and forget this sorry episode. I don't want to go away with you for a few days' break. I think it would be best for you and for me if I book a flight home tomorrow.'

'No! You started this, so you should have the decency to finish it! Tell me what was so important for you to go to all this trouble. I still suggest that you and I go away for a few days before we part yet again.'

'Okay, but you have to hear me out! Do not interrupt me!' I demanded. And I said what I had come to say: 'I am to marry Donald at the end of next month. I do not love him in the way that I love you. You are to marry Susan next month, and I believe that you do not love Susan the way that you love me. I decided that I had to give us – that is, you and me – one last chance before it was too late for either of us.' I waited for a reaction from Thomas, but there was none.

'Thomas Hague, will you marry me? Take me to Vegas and marry me now. To hell with everybody else.' Still, there was no reaction from Thomas, but I did notice that he hesitated. 'You hesitated, Thomas. Please do not let me go,' I pleaded with him.

'I'm sorry, Catherine. I have to go through with my wedding. Susan's family are prepared to back me all the way in my race for the senate, and they are not the sort of people that you mess around with.'

'I know. I just thought that I really had to give us one final last chance at happiness before it was too late. Never mind. I knew it was a long shot, so I will be going home, and you will never hear from me or see me again.' I spoke quietly.

'So you and Donald. I am not surprised. He is wealthy, and he will be able to take good care of you,' said a thoughtful Thomas.

'Don't be so sanctimonious! Do you not realize how important all this is to me, and of course, to you?' I retaliated. Again, I said, 'Thomas Hague, will you marry me? Take me to Vegas and marry me now, before it is too late for either of us.'

We were both silent for a little while.

'I am going to phone Annie and tell her to pack me a bag before Susan gets back from the church. She can bring it here to the hotel. I will not take no for an answer. We are going to go away for a week or so, not just a few days. If it makes you feel any better, I promise that we shall both keep in touch with each other from now on.' He seemed very upset.

I wondered how I was going to explain to Donald that I was going to be away for a week or so. How was I going to tell him where I was? Also, how was Thomas going to explain to Susan why he had gone away with me? Paul, her brother, was bound to tell her that he had seen us together – holding hands!

After the meal, we strolled back to the hotel. We walked through the small park, and as before, I hugged Thomas's arm. We kissed. We laughed. We acted like lovers, but my heart was breaking!

As we neared the hotel, I saw Annie standing by a car. She waved to me, and when I reached her, we held each other.

Annie seemed very upset at seeing me again after such a long time. Thomas instructed her not to tell anybody about us going away. If anybody insisted on knowing where we had gone, she was to tell them that we had set off to Long Island, probably on the boat. After Thomas had retrieved his bag, Annie left.

Back in the hotel room, Thomas told me that he was very concerned about Susan and her family stopping us from leaving together, so he thought it might be a good idea if we left for Santa Barbara early in the morning.

'You get some sleep. I have an hour's work to do. Just make sure you are packed and ready to go.' Thomas laughed.

I was so tired that, once I curled up on the bed, I fell fast asleep.

It was two o'clock in the morning when Thomas woke me. He had brought me a coffee from reception, and he said that he had checked us out and told the reception that we were heading for Long Island. I presumed that was in case anyone came asking for details of where we might have gone. It all seemed a little cloak and dagger, but as long as I was with Thomas, I just went along with any arrangements he had made.

We collected my suitcase, and Thomas settled me down in the passenger seat with a lovely woollen rug wrapped around me to keep me cosy and warm.

'You go back to sleep. I will wake you when we are nearly there,' said Thomas as he held me close and kissed me. We then drove away.

It did not take much for me to settle down, all wrapped up and cosy. I watched all the traffic on the freeway. Even at that time in the morning, LA was a buzzing place. I drifted back to sleep.

Sometime later, I opened my eyes. The radio was playing love songs into the night. I looked outside the car window. There were no cars on the highway. There were no streetlights; everywhere was really dark. I looked at Thomas, and he just smiled back at me and carried on driving. I was feeling so low, and I was feeling defeated.

Thomas was driving quite fast, but for a split second, I saw a road sign as we passed. I thought it read 'Barstow.' I turned to Thomas, and he returned my look and winked at me. *Oh my God!* My heart started to beat so loudly. I was almost too afraid to ask Thomas if we were on our way to Vegas. 'Are you going to tell me that we are on our way to Vegas to get married?' I whispered.

'No, I am not, but those papers there on the backseat might provide some clues!' Thomas laughed.

I grabbed the papers. There were three of them. The first one was a confirmation of a hotel booking at The Venetian, a beautiful hotel on the Strip in Vegas. The second was a booking for a marriage service at the Candlelight Chapel in Vegas for eleven in the morning. The third was a Nevada marriage licence in the names of Catherine Riding and Thomas Hague. I shook from head to foot. I was in total shock. Then, I put my face into my hands and broke down and cried.

'For goodness sake, Catherine, please, please do not cry. Save all your energy for getting through today. As long as the minister is not told of my other marriage booking, we shall be Mr. and Mrs. Hague by lunchtime today. I am just hoping that no one has realized that we are getting married today. I am supposed to be making you happy, so why all the tears?'

'When did you decide to marry me?' I asked as I tried to stop sobbing.

'As soon as you asked me, I phoned Annie and told her to empty my safe. I told her to remove all the legal documents and all the money I kept in there. I told her to lock the safe again and place all the papers, money, and some clothes into a bag. I told her to make sure she packed my best summer suit, a fancy shirt, and my shoes that matched. She knew then what I was planning, and she had such a shock when she saw you. That is why she broke down and cried. What is it with you women? When something good is going down, you all have to cry?' He laughed, and I laughed with him through my tears.

'Thomas, I will love you forever and a day. I promise to make you very happy, as well as making myself happy too. I am so excited I cannot think straight. It has been such a shock. Are you sure that I am not dreaming this?' I asked, still sobbing.

'Well, if you are dreaming this, then I am dreaming this as well.' He then pulled into the forecourt of a tourist information centre for Las Vegas.

'I presume a visit to the rest rooms would be a good idea now. I am going to ask the folks here about what they can do to help us with our wedding arrangements. They might just come up with an idea or two.' We walked indoors.

Thomas was correct. They offered us the use of a wedding limo, which Thomas booked. The limo would collect us from the rear entrance of The Venetian at ten thirty in the morning. We had the use of the limo until evening. Nothing else that they offered us was appropriate, but the limo was a great idea.

Back in the car, we drove straight to the hotel. While Thomas was booking us in, I made my way into the accessories shop. I purchased a large cerise flower and a long cerise silk scarf.

The hotel room was fabulous, with one massive king-size bed. The room was actually a suite, complete with a separate lounge area with television, computer, and games console. Not that we would be playing any games! We would have better things to do.

Thomas ordered a breakfast from room service, and while we were rushing to get dressed as quickly as possible, we were eating our breakfasts and drinking coffee. We treated ourselves to a large brandy from the room bar. We laughed, we talked, and we kissed while I tried to help Thomas get dressed in his fancy shirt and suit, and Thomas tried to help me get dressed in my cream dress, to which I attached the large cerise flower. I used the silk scarf as a belt, wrapping it around my waist, hanging it to the side of my dress. I finished my outfit with fancy jewellery and fancy shoes. I did not forget to put my suspender and stockings on with small fancy knickers. We laughed as Thomas tried to mess about with me sexually, and my answer to that was a definite *no*.

'We are not even married yet, and you are saying no to my sexual advances? Just wait until you are Mrs. Hague. There will be no saying no then!' We laughed as we kissed and held each other as close as could be.

'We shall have some very upsetting phone calls to make after the wedding, but we must not let the thought of those phone calls stop us from enjoying our day!' instructed Thomas.

***

We left the hotel via the rear entrance to find our wedding limo waiting for us. In no time at all, we were in the Candlelight Chapel. All the paperwork was completed. We chose two wedding rings from the rings at the chapel gift shop. They were platinum with diamond chips. I had a small bottle of Lourdes holy water, which I always carried with me. I used it to bless the rings.

It all happened so quickly. All I could really remember were the words, 'I now pronounce you husband and wife.' We kissed briefly and made our way out after collecting two original marriage certificates, one for Thomas and one for me.

As we got back into the limo, we held each other tight. 'Never let go of me, Thomas!' I whispered.

'I shall never let go of you. My arms are around you, and I am holding you tight. I shall hold you tight for the rest of our lives. I love you so much. I will never let you down, Catherine!'

'Right, now for our honeymoon!' said a very serious Thomas. 'I suggest that we have a wedding lunch at Lake Mead. We shall feed the large carp fish. They fascinate me when they all come to the surface. From now on, Mrs. Hague, we shall enjoy ourselves all the time. There will be no sadness in our lives. I have no idea where we shall live. I have no idea what we are going to do with ourselves. All I do know is that we are now on a journey together. Nobody will ever separate us again.'

'Thomas Hague, my beautiful Thomas Hague, as long as you are always holding me tight, I shall love you forever and a day!' I whispered as I kissed and held my new husband tight.

Always in my heart, let love be my judge.

About the Author

Marion Catterall lives in the northwest of England and was educated at the Convent of the Holy Child Jesus in Preston, Lancashire. Since she was a young woman, she wanted to write novels. She started a few stories but never finished because life got in the way. However, she has now written two novels. For years, she ran her own haulage business. She is married and has children and grandchildren.

About the Book

Whilst in America, a middle-aged woman meets and starts a relationship with an American judge. After returning to England, she meets and starts a relationship with a Scottish laird. Torn between the love of two beautiful men, she must make heartbreaking decisions. The descriptive sexual content in this book demonstrates the love, desire, passion, pleasure, and emotion that produces the drama of the situations she finds herself in.